Forever The One.com

by

Connie Y Harris

The Forever Series, Book Three

Cover Art by *Kristian Norris*

The Wild Rose Press, Inc.
PO Box 708
Adams Basin, NY 14410-0708
Visit us at www.thewildrosepress.com

Publishing History
First Edition, 2024
Trade Paperback ISBN 978-1-5092-5451-4
Digital ISBN 978-1-5092-5452-1

The Forever Series, Book Three
Published in the United States of America

Dedication

This book is dedicated to my nephew, John, a disabled veteran, devoted husband and father, and the bravest man I know. To his loving wife, Marci, who deserves flowers and chocolates forever for always having John's back. And to the dedicated game wardens of Texas, with a special thanks to Angel Miller, keep up the professional job you perform daily. I'm grateful for your service.

Chapter One

Mariah Michaels gunned the engine of her twenty-eighteen four-by-four, dodging sporadic potholes as she sped along one of the many backcountry roads in East Texas. Dust swirled behind the truck, creating a thick mass of red particles, making the visibility from her rear-view mirror impossible. She checked the side mirror. A black Suburban slid into momentary view, then disappeared. *Too close for comfort and gaining on me.* The tricked-out vehicle with dark tinted windows reminded her of ones she'd impounded after discovering drugs stuffed in the interior walls. Not that she sought that kind of arrest, but as a law enforcement officer, an illegal transaction obligated her to act. The screen on her cell phone lit up. She glanced at the caller ID. *Mama? What now?* Her mind raced as she fumbled for the phone. *I should hit decline. But what if it's an emergency?*

"Hi, Mama," she said, forcing calm into her tone, aware any strain in her voice might betray her apprehension of who the hell was barreling up her tailpipe. "Everything okay?"

"Not by a long shot. I can't find the remote and my show, "Naked and Afraid" is about to come on."

Mariah white-knuckled the steering wheel to keep from screaming. Her mother's memory lapses were getting worse. "Did you check the coffee table?" Her eyes flicked to the rear-view mirror.

"Yes." Her mama's voice wobbled. "I could have sworn I left the blasted thing in the living room, but it's not there." Then she whispered, "Someone must have moved it."

"Okay, Mama. I'll come over after work and we'll make a checklist together of possible places the remote would be."

In a barely audible voice, she asked, "What if someone stole it?"

Mariah swallowed the burning liquid surging up her throat and replied, "I'll arrest them."

She glanced again in the rear-view and was startled to see the vehicle directly behind her. Whoever this was, weaving back and forth, meant to send a message and scare the bejesus out of her. Mission accomplished.

"Gotta go Mama. Ask Franny if you can watch your show at her house. I'll call you later."

"Good idea, honey. Be safe. Goodbye."

In the split second that followed, the heavy SUV rammed her rear bumper with enough force to snap her neck backward, jerk it forward, then slam it against the headrest. Mariah braced her back against the seat as the truck skidded onto the raised shoulder. Stunned, she gripped the wheel and righted the tires back onto the dirt road.

She thumbed the transmit button of her radio. "This is Bravo W 22." Exhaling a jagged breath, she continued, "1033, rammed by an SUV, speed of seventy miles per hour while trying to elude. Requesting any available units in response area for backup on unpaved road, two miles Northeast of CR One."

A voice from the dispatcher crackled over the radio. "You okay, Bravo W? I checked and the closest sheriff is ETA two minutes out, at the boat dock near Eagle Mountain Lake."

"For now. The driver gave me a hard tap on my bumper. Flipped me up on the berm, but I'm back on the road, 10-17 for the dock."

"Any ID?"

"Can't g-get physical description of occupants at this time." The stutter in her voice betrayed her attempt to sound unruffled.

"Sounds like you need help now. I'll radio the sheriff to intercept."

"Ten-four, dispatch. One mile out." She eyed the straight stretch of road ahead, gripped the wheel and stomped on the gas pedal. After a quick glance in the rear-view, she inhaled a deep breath and sighed in relief as the black SUV receded behind a screen of sand and dirt kicked up by the all-terrain tires on her truck. She maintained her speed until the dock came into view. A sheriff's sedan, parked next to the gravel ramp, flashed blue and red lights. The passenger side door was open. A twenty-something deputy stood braced against the frame with his gun drawn. As she slowed, he gave an emphatic wave indicating she should shift to the right, near the tree line. *What?*

The retort of gunfire startled her into action as the windshield of the deputy's patrol car shattered. The deputy instantly returned fire. She whipped the wheel to the right, drove onto the dried grass sideways, and slammed on the brakes. Twisted to the left, she slipped her hand through the crack in the seat and rifled around the floorboard for her hard body armor. With rapid gun fire ripping past her, she crawled out the passenger side and crouched on the ground, slipping the additional armor over her bullet-proof vest. There was no way to retrieve her Bushmaster fully automatic rifle. She clutched the holster slung low on her hip. The forty-caliber Glock would have to do.

Peeking over the hood of her truck, she viewed a chaotic scene. The black SUV didn't slow down as it barreled up to the dock but continued in a semi-circle as two shooters fired from the back seat. A sudden hiss and tilt down of her truck signaled her tire had taken a round. *Damn.* She aimed and fired at the shooter closest to her. He winced as he simultaneously grabbed his arm and fell backward in the car. After making a full turn, they sped down the road toward the highway.

She memorized the license number before holstering her weapon, then, with her thumb clamped on the transmit button, she recited the tag to the dispatcher along with a request for an APB.

With her head on a swivel, she crabbed sideways to the officer's position. "Are you okay?"

"Yep." He holstered his gun and stuck out his hand. "Luke Story."

"Mariah Michaels." She returned his firm grip. "Thanks for the backup."

"No problem." He shook his head, sending small flecks of glass to the ground. "Who were those guys?"

"You got me, but I called in an APB with their tag number and…." Interrupted by the crackle of her radio, she held up a finger and pushed the button. "Dispatch, go ahead."

She hugged the radio close to her ear while the dispatcher talked. "Ran the tags."

"And?" She glanced at Officer Story and raised her eyebrows.

"Stolen," the dispatcher replied.

Mariah shook her head, then said, "Ten-four."

Before she could share the call, Luke said, "Let me guess, stolen tags?"

She nodded, then quickly assessed the damage to their vehicles, before adding, "We're going to need a tow truck."

He stooped to pick up an empty cartridge. "And a forensic team," he added.

****

John Armstrong rolled his wheelchair up the ramp to his two-bedroom cottage and home since being released from care at the Tampa, Florida Veteran's Center. After several months in a coma, John woke up to the memory of lying under a flipped Humvee after an IED exploded and the realization he'd been severely injured. But how badly? The doctor dropped the bomb he'd be in a wheelchair for the rest of his life. There was hope of increased mobility with physical therapy but…. His mind had gone numb. His life, as he had lived it, was over.

His sister, Ariel, insisted he move onto the Ocala, Florida horse farm where she lived with her husband, Gavin Cross, a former Navy SEAL. After his father died, Gavin traded in his SEAL Trident for jeans and a pair of cowboy boots. Along with Ariel, an equine vet, they managed one of the most prestigious thoroughbred racehorse farms in America.

Life on the farm had its benefits. His treatment plan from the VA included water therapy, and the Olympic-sized swimming pool served as a cool retreat in the blistering summer heat. Home-cooked meals by the long-term family housekeeper, Bessie Mae, beat any restaurant food in the area and his service dog, Cosmo, had acres in which to roam, although the German Shepherd never left his side. But there wasn't much social life in the country. Bottom line, he was lonely. He longed for a relationship with a good woman, a partner to share his life, someone who'd love him despite his disability. Was she out there? He didn't know, but he'd continue the search and hope.

Which is why joining a dating site seemed like a good idea. Some of his Marine buddies suggested ForeverTheOne.com. They even peered over his shoulder while they drank beer and made rude suggestions as he set up a profile. Over his strenuous objections, they posted pictures of him in front of his sister's expansive main house with pastured horses in the background, giving viewers an impression of wealth. He got a plethora of responses. In the military, John served as an expert in surveillance and reconnaissance, which he hoped would help him weed out the gold diggers and crazies, but a few slipped through.

"Hey, bud, how did your date go last night?" Ariel stepped into his home office, a stainless-steel tumbler in her hand. She leaned over and rubbed Cosmo's ears. He welcomed her with a lick.

John shrugged. "Typical. The profile picture was obviously air-brushed. Emails went back and forth but when we met, yikes."

Ariel screwed up her face. "What happened?"

"My date showed up at Ocean Prime restaurant wearing torn jeans, you know, like the ones with the knee material missing, a wrinkled t-shirt, hair teased, and bright red lipstick. If I could run," he huffed, "I would have." He lifted his head and caught her wide-eyed expression.

"Oh, John, I'm so sorry." Ariel stepped behind the wheelchair and rested her free hand on his shoulder. "I'm afraid to ask. How did dinner go?"

He shrugged. "She gulped wine between bites of shoveled food, used her biscuits to wipe the plate clean, and asked for extra biscuits in a to-go box. Sis, I swear, I was back in the army mess hall instead of fine dining at a five-star eatery."

"Let me guess. You were a perfect gentleman and picked up the tab?" She sipped from the tumbler, then laid it on the table.

"Yep. My big sister trained me well." He backed his wheelchair in a sharp turn to face her, a boyish grin on his face. "On the bright side, she wasn't as bad as the bunny lady."

"Oh no, not the bunny lady." With her hands holding her sides, Ariel caught her breath between outbursts of laughter. "How can one woman own so many rabbits?"

"I told you how," John said, nodding his head. "Let them hop unchecked all over your house, doing the thing they love most, humping like bunnies. That's how."

Normally, his dates requested he meet them in public, at a restaurant or coffee shop. This woman asked him to pick her up at her house. When he arrived, the first big surprise was the ramp attached to her front porch. Curious. She didn't mention having a disability. After he entered the house, he realized the problem wasn't physical. Stacks of newspapers filled every recess of the living room and the pungent smell of bunny poop, well, gagged him. Clumps of fur formed nests beside the fireplace, under the drapes…. A flash of white hopped by followed by a flash of brown, then black. Oh hell, rabbits. Everywhere. The black one hopped up to him and sniffed his chair, then nibbled his pants. With its nose twitching in the air, he thumped his leg, obviously initiating Morse code for back-up as suddenly fifty bunnies surrounded his wheelchair, grunting, whimpering, and yes, screaming at his intrusion. His date had disappeared into the kitchen, so he stealthily retreated out of the house, careful not to roll over any bunny toes, and sped out of the driveway without a second glance back.

Ariel hugged her waist, laughing. "Stop. Please stop. I'll never get this story out of my head." She clamped her lips together in an apparent attempt to stifle her giggles.

John loved making his sister laugh. Aside from the security work he did for the family farm and other horse farms in Ocala, his real mission in life was to repay her complete devotion to him after his accident. She gave up a career-bolstering move to Lexington and a chance to practice medicine at the most prestigious Thoroughbred horse farm in the world to supervise his recovery. So, he'd continue to entertain her with his dating fails if it made her happy. "Hey, I've got plenty more. You up for it?"

She righted herself and slid her palms down her pant legs, vigorously shaking her head. "No." She inhaled a deep breath. "I'm good." Then, she tousled his hair and sat in a chair adjacent to him. "On a more serious note, is there any news about the horse murders at Wellington Farms?"

"The surveillance camera picked up a middle-aged man in a dark hoodie leading a horse out of the barn." He shook his head. "Thing is…the horse went willingly. He trusted that scumbag."

"Yes, they're flight animals and in the wild will flee if confronted by a predator, but we humans have conditioned them to trust us."

"Sis, the gelding in the video was found in a wooded area, skinned before being partially butchered."

Ariel instinctively glanced out the window toward the barn, then continued. "Unfortunately, the high demand for horse meat in some overseas countries makes savaging these beautiful creatures very lucrative."

"I've already turned in the video to the sheriff. They'll catch this guy."

"Or guys…as in crime syndicate," she added, chewing the corner of her index finger.

"Hey," John slapped at her finger, "I know animal cruelty stresses you out but gnawing your finger off won't help catch these guys."

"Ugh. What they're doing is so blatant and awful, but you're right." Ariel dropped her hand. "Bad habit." She pointed to the computer screen as she leaned in, peering over his shoulder. "Who is that?"

"You mean the blonde babe who is totally out of my league?"

"It says perfect match and yes, she's beautiful but certainly not out of your league, my hot baby brother." She thumped him on the back of the head.

"Ouch!" He rubbed his head. "That's Mariah

Michaels from Ft Worth, Texas."

"She's wearing a uniform and badge. Law enforcement?"

Reading aloud, John said, "Game Warden, so yes. Also, single, never married, and no children." He angled his wheelchair to record her reaction. "No baggage."

"Wait just a little minute." Ariel flattened her hand on her belly and circled the rounded baby bump before pointing to her stomach. "He's not baggage." She then waggled her finger at him. "Wait until you have your own." She kissed her fingers and rested them on her stomach.

"Elmo's my nephew. That's different." He raised his eyebrows. "He's my blood."

"Tsk. Tsk. Tsk. I already told you NO on the name Elmo." She waggled her finger at him again, this time harder, and laughed.

"That's a strong name," he said in mocked protest.

"No, little brother. It's the name of a goofy red puppet who likes to be tickled."

"You're no fun." He snorted with laughter. "And I don't view kids as baggage."

"All kidding aside, we agreed this little nugget will be named in memory of our father."

John grabbed her hand. "Mom was pregnant with me when dad died serving as a Marine." He squeezed. "You sure you want him to bear the onus of the past?"

"My husband isn't going back into the military." She positioned her index fingers in the sign of a cross. This little one will be blessed, not cursed by his grandfather's legacy."

John gazed at his limp legs. He joined the Marines

after college and deployed to Afghanistan. Not exactly the outcome he'd expected. Dark memories swept and reminded him who bore the baggage. He started to speak but decided against anymore downer talk. Instead, he turned his wheelchair and his attention back toward the screen. Hopeful of inspiring more banter with his sister, he overlayed Mariah's page with an Elmo emoji.

"I'm ignoring that ridiculous hint, little brother," Ariel said, her arms lightly resting on his back. "Are you going to send her a thumbs up or whatever it is you do to take it to the next level?"

"Considering the parade of gold diggers, fakers, and fashion-challenged who have pursued me, combined with the minefield of technical jargon, I might shut it all down."

"Hmm," Ariel reacted as she read silently. "This Mariah person has a straightforward bio and seems professional. There's no talk of bread crumbing, or pansexual."

John rolled his eyes.

"Not-judging," she said. "Just saying….Give her a wink."

"I'll send her an email," he retorted, then tucked his wheelchair under the desk. He typed until his office door closed with a click. Then, with his finger suspended over the delete button, he reviewed the game warden's bio. *I'm making a fool of myself. She's not going to want me.* He stared at the curvy female image with the endless blonde ponytail. *Brains and beauty, Even ForeverTheOne.com agrees she's my ideal match.* As his finger hovered over the keyboard, his hand started to shake. *Without risk, there is no reward.* He punched 'send'.

Chapter Two

Shades of evening cast shadows along the sidewalk as Mariah arrived, exhausted and frustrated at the card reader outside the Laurel Hills apartment complex. She backed her rental car into her assigned parking space and shifted into Park. A gated community near the station offered the needed security and convenience for her while she saved money for her first house. She even agreed to a roommate, although reluctantly.

As she unbuckled her seat belt, a ding on her phone caught her attention. An email from someone on the dating site she joined, had downloaded. Admittedly, dating sites weren't really her thing but her work schedule and office-in-a-car workspace offered limited opportunity to meet any single guys. She scanned the note. *Nice, straightforward.* The name at the end, John Armstrong, rang a bell. *No harm in checking out his profile.* A sudden movement next to her door grabbed her attention, sending a sharp spasm of fear cascading through her body. She grabbed her gun but relaxed when her quirky roommate, Tisdale Maude Barnette, pressed her face against the closed window, thumbs in ears, waving her fingers like a three-year-old.

Mariah rolled down the window, her face scrunched in a frown. "You scared me, Tizzy."

"I didn't mean to," she simpered. "You had your face stuck in that phone so hard you didn't see me waving to you from the porch." She glanced up to the second-story walkway. "You also didn't notice me strolling through the parking lot. You usually possess much more of an eagle eye. What gives?" she asked, then stuck the fingers of her right hand in her mouth and chewed on her nails.

Mariah tapped the back arrow on the screen twice. "Nothing. Tough day." Tizzy, as she liked to be called, was harmless but nosy, and, if allowed, would give any advice columnist a run for her money.

Tizzy opened the car door. Mariah dropped her phone in her purse, then draped the leather strap over her shoulder before handing Tizzy her computer and exiting her seat with a forward thrust.

"I fixed dinner and made extra. You hungry?" Tizzy asked as she snatched the laptop balanced on Mariah's arm.

"Thanks for the offer but I have a lot of forms to fill out before I report to work tomorrow." She yawned, then shook it off. "I'll probably skip food tonight and head for bed as soon as humanly possible."

The curve of Tizzy's lips reversed from a smile to a pout. Mariah, not wanting to seem ungrateful, quickly added, "You know what? I think I could use a bite to eat while I fill out my paperwork."

Tizzy's smile returned. While she bounced up the stairs, Mariah hung back and scanned the parking lot. No sign of anyone lurking. She extended her view to the tree line and observed nothing unusual. All quiet on that front. With a final glance toward the wood line, she continued up the stairs to the top and her front door. She still couldn't reconcile what happened earlier, but whoever it was hadn't followed her here. Regardless,

Tizzy was correct. She needed to up her situational awareness. With her right foot, she nudged the door closed. A good night's sleep and a quick bite to eat would go a long way in remedying her restless mind.

She kicked off her dusty work boots and unpacked her gear, setting her phone and gun on the bedside table before retreating to the adjoining bathroom. Too tired to take a shower she used makeup removing wipes to cleanse the day's dirt off her face. She closed her eyes and inhaled the scent of fresh cucumbers as the soft, cool cloth brushed against her skin. A soft tap, tap, tap on her bedroom door reminded her Tizzy had prepared dinner and she'd agreed to join her.

"Coming," she called out. She shuffled to the bedroom door and twisted the doorknob.

A familiar giggle erupted from the other side. Prepared for one of the common pranks her roommate liked to play, she yanked open the door. Tizzy took a step back, then clapped her hands and bounced up and down. Mariah glanced in both directions, checking for Tizzy's source of excitement, then stepped forward. A hot, thick substance oozed between her toes.

"What the…!" She yelled, while instinctively withdrawing her foot and vigorously shaking it. Teaspoon-sized flecks of mashed potato splattered the surrounding furniture.

"Oh no," Tizzy moaned. "I'm so sorry, Mariah." She bent over to recover the tray of food she'd left at the door. "I wanted to surprise you."

"Well, you did that," Mariah said between tightly pursed lips. She lowered her foot and allowed what was left of the creamy goo to settle into the carpet. "What a mess." She frowned and shook her head as she surveyed the damage then checked her watch. "No rest for the weary. This will take at least an hour to clean up."

Tizzy's face, now tinged with a bright red flush, said, "I *am* sorry." She set the tray on a nearby chair, then hurried into the kitchen where she retrieved a roll of paper towels.

"I'll clean it up," she said with a shaky voice as she knelt in front of Mariah and tore off several sheets.

"Thanks," Mariah said, softening her tone. "I'll help." She accepted the offered roll. "I admit. I'm tired and cranky." She wiped the potatoes from her toes. "But I do appreciate the gesture." She observed Tizzy as she buzzed erratically around the apartment. "Question, and please don't take this the wrong way, but you seem a bit wired. Did you take your meds today?"

Tizzy halted her cleaning and gazed up at Mariah. "The Xanax?" Her eyes shifted down. "No. I forgot. I haven't taken it for days. It makes me so groggy and lethargic."

Mariah knelt at eye level with her roommate and placed her hand on Tizzy's shoulder. "The psychiatrist prescribed the drug for a reason, Tisdale."

"I know. My anxiety." She clamped her teeth on her bottom lip. "I don't know which is worse—my manic, paranoid attitude if I don't take the prescription, or the walking dead mood if I do."

"Well, I suggest you make an appointment with the doctor and explain your concerns. Maybe he'll change or even adjust the medication."

Tizzy offered Mariah a weak smile and a nod. She retrieved the food tray and held it out to Mariah. "That was the last of the mashed, but you've still got the meatloaf."

"The meatloaf smells yummy. It'll be plenty." Mariah smiled. "Thanks again."

"Enjoy," Tizzy replied as she returned to the cleanup. "Go eat. I'll finish here."

Mariah lifted the tray to her nose and inhaled the spicy aroma. *Hmm. I am hungry*. Her stomach growled in response. After retreating into her bedroom, she placed the tray on a table while she opened her laptop and searched the dating site for John Armstrong's profile. *Voila*. Retrieving the tray, she heaved the first bite into her mouth as she perused the pictures and bio. "Impressive guy. A little on the young side. But are you real?" She scrutinized his picture some more. "And why me?" She exited the screen and put his name in a search bar. "Holy fishing without a license."

****

John's breath hitched as he opened his profile and an email downloaded. With surging anxiety, he opened the game warden's reply and skimmed the first few words, expecting the sting of rejection. "I don't date guys in wheelchairs. You're not my type. Was hoping for a musician." But his perusal slowed as his pulse quickened. *She asked questions. She wants a reply*. John slapped the arms of his wheelchair. Cosmo, asleep by his side, sat up, his steady gaze fixed on his owner. John bent forward and cupped the dog's face in his hands. "She's interested, buddy." Cosmo's tail wagged in a vigorous back-and-forth motion.

Happy, John patted the top of Cosmo's head while his mouth stretched in a too-long-absent grin. Not sure why this female, whom he'd never met face to face and didn't really know, intrigued him. But he'd follow his gut and rather than play it cool and wait a couple of days to respond, he'd go all in and answer right away. As in now.

The first thing she did was thank him for his service. *My pleasure.* The next words she wrote jolted him. "Never Forget." He'd never experienced this kind of sincerity and intensity about his military service from other potential matches. It wasn't all about her. Nor did it feel like a polite acknowledgement or the politically correct thing to say. The words impinged like a wrecking ball. Then she asked him questions. "What hobbies do you have? Do you like horses? Have you ever visited Texas?"

As he stared out the window at the succession of white picket fences encircling rich, green pastures, dotted with million-dollar horses, his memories drifted back to a different time in an ancient place, Kandahar valley in Afghanistan. Not peaceful and pastoral like what he viewed from this window but beautifully rustic in an undefined, wild way.

Assigned as the officer in charge of a Marine recon mission, he rode in the lead Humvee. A Navy SEAL sniper acting as point man was positioned on the hood when an IED they rolled over exploded. The blast somersaulted the vehicle and pinned him under its heavy metal frame. With sniper fire from the enemy pinging around his head, he fought to stay conscious, focusing on the male voice calling to him from nearby. *I'm here, lieutenant. I'll get you out.* The point man fired back at the sniper. Then, the shooting stopped. The SEAL called for air rescue and repeated the words, *flight medic* over and over. His world spun into blackness and stayed there for many months afterward. In an instant, his life drastically changed. The bright military future everyone agreed was his for the asking, evaporated. Now confined to a wheelchair, he struggled daily with depression. He hated the idea of being a victim and, worse, being a burden to his sister and her husband. Or anyone. His shoulders shook as tears spilled down his cheeks. He swiped them away as fast as they appeared. Cosmo laid his chin in John's lap, his soulful amber eyes peered up to his master's face.

"I'm not ready, Cosmo," John said, choking back a sob. Cosmo stepped back as John grabbed the rail of the spoked wheels and spun them forward toward the large, metal button beside the door. He slammed his palm on the word *push,* and called for Cosmo to come. The door swung out and Cosmo, who normally darted ahead, paused as John raced down the ramp, his muscular arms pumping in a furious circular motion.

Chapter Three

Mariah printed off the results of the online search and stuffed it in her back pocket. As she dressed for work, she contemplated whether she should share her findings with Tizzy. A mutual friend introduced them about a year ago at an outdoor fish fry. She seemed sweet and when it became apparent the only way Mariah could afford a future house was to have a roommate share her living expenses now, Tizzy was the first person she contacted. In the beginning, the arrangement benefited each of them equally, but lately, the roommate scale tilted in Tizzy's favor. She wanted more together time than Mariah's schedule would allow and took it personally when Mariah said she had other plans. Yep. Better not give her anything that would incite resentment. She grabbed her personal laptop and decided to use her lunch hour to check for a response to her questions. This John Armstrong guy showed promise.

Her office was a large, new trailer behind the Tarrant County Law Enforcement Center. Space was at a premium in the complex, so her team got shuffled out to one of the brand-new overflow trailers. She didn't need fancy to do her job. In fact, she preferred the trailer, as it gave her privacy. There were only five game wardens to cover all of Tarrant County, so she usually had plenty of alone time at her desk. Like right now. She checked the yard in front of her desk window. Empty. She tilted onto her right hip and slid the piece of paper from her back pocket. John Armstrong's military headshot showed a handsome, dark-haired, hazel-eyed man in his twenties with a confident grin. The insignia pinned on his uniform collar belonged to the rank of lieutenant. She skimmed the details of his education and training, then slowed as the article recounted the particulars of his last mission.

"Such a tragedy," she whispered. "He's lucky to be alive." She swiped at moisture slipping out and over the corner of her eye, then shifted her gaze up to his face. The face of a confident military man. She scrolled back to the photo on the profile page and realized the discrepancy. The eyes in the website image portrayed a lack of sparkle that results from a loss of innocence. She'd never served in the military, but most of her male counterparts had and on the many long drives through the Texas countryside she'd learned how to listen. John's story was one she wanted to hear. She set up her laptop, opened the Yahoo window, and reviewed all the downloaded emails. *Hmm. No response…yet.* She'd give him another day.

The crunch of gravel outside sucked her attention away from the computer screen. She peered out the window in time to return the wave from her supervisor as he rolled up in his agency car. Frank was what she referred to as a grizzled old veteran. Born and raised in Texas with twenty years as a game warden, there wasn't much he didn't know and little that surprised him. Still, she kept her personal life to herself. She slid the paper under her laptop and closed the browser before sidestepping to open the trailer door.

"Hey, Captain." She welcomed him with a bright smile as she held the door ajar.

His gruff demeanor softened. "How's it going, Mariah?"

"No complaints."

"I heard about your encounter." He thumbed in the direction of her rental car parked outside. "Other than your truck, any personal injury?" He scanned her body with an avuncular concern.

"Nope. All good." She rocked back on the heels of her weathered, leather work boots, uncomfortable recalling 'the encounter' as he called it. She wondered where this line of questioning was headed. Did it fall under his duties as an internal investigation? Or was it simply concern for his protégé?

"I've requested Sheriff Hardy's office investigate the incident with all available resources." He stared at the carpeted floor. His brow furrowed for a full minute before lifting his head. "I don't believe for a second this was some isolated attack. Someone's trying to scare you…or worse."

"But—"

Frank raised his hand. "I won't have my agents intimidated, for god's sake."

Touched by his concern, she simply nodded.

"I've arranged for your truck to be driven here this afternoon," —his demeanor eased— "with all new tires."

She tilted her head. "Only one was shot out?"

He smiled. "I know, but with the roads you travel, and the rubber you burn, tires wear out fast."

She snorted. "Thank you, sir."

He veered toward the door, then stopped. "By the

way, the rumor mill is buzzing with reports of imminent orders for game wardens to assist border agents with the influx of illegal migrants crossing through gaps in the wall."

"Really? I stay busy handing out tickets for fishing and hunting infractions." She wrinkled her nose. "Now, I'm chasing coyotes and drug smugglers?"

"You're law enforcement here in Texas. Have a bag packed and be ready to go at a moment's notice." He offered a quick salute. "And be careful," he added over his shoulder as he exited down the stairs.

"Will do," she said as the door slammed shut.

Before she could absorb the magnitude of what an assist to border agents might include, the phone on her desk rang. Anxious for something normal like an injured owl or a wild boar sighting, she sprang to grab the call. "Agent Michaels here."

Silence, then slow, heavy breathing, followed by a click. She gawked at the receiver before dropping it back in the cradle as if she'd received a jolt of electricity. *What a pervert.* She picked the receiver back up and dialed the operator. "Can you tell what number the last call came from?"

"No, but it was a female reporting possible poachers on a side road to Highway Eighty-Seven, so I put it through. Is there a problem?"

"No. We got disconnected, so if she calls back, get her name and number."

"You got it." The operator ended the call.

Mariah checked her watch and noticed her hand was shaking. *A female? I don't get it.* She tightened her ponytail and straightened the papers on her desk. An uneventful night, hours before, now unsettled her. The main law enforcement building, located across the parking lot, was a short distance away, but when a shiver shook her entire body, the realization she was isolated collapsed her false bravado. She glanced at the entrance and noticed the position of the deadbolt was upright. With a quick hop to the door, she secured the lock and then stepped backward to her desk. She needed to shift her attention back on work. When she reopened her laptop and clicked on emails, a plethora of agency-related dispatches downloaded.

Great. Much-needed distraction.

The last email had a familiar address. She held her breath while it opened. John Armstrong sent her a request to Skype. He didn't answer any of her questions but simply asked for a live face-to-face that evening. Intrigued, she typed, yes and hit send.

Chapter Four

Together, John and Cosmo careened down the hard-packed path past the main house and the barns to the wooden pier stretching out from the bank of the freshwater lake. Gavin had built an access ramp for John. He rolled up to it and stopped, motioning for Cosmo to sit. There were ramps installed all over the property for him because, per Gavin, John's experience on the farm needed as few limitations as possible. His sister and brother-in-law worked hard to make his life comfortable, and they deserved his gratitude. He even owed Gavin his life. More than once, the guy had exposed himself to life-threatening situations to save his ass. *Then why does the urge to roll off the end of this pier creep into my consciousness?* He stared at his limp legs, then slapped them with the flat of his palms. *I don't feel a thing. Nothing but deadness. I don't want to be a burden.*

The recent barn fire crossed his mind. After his sister's crazy ex set the barn on fire and locked him inside, Gavin's heroic rescue prevented him from succumbing to smoke inhalation. Maybe better for everyone if his brother-in-law had let him die in the fire.

John kept his daily battles with depression a secret. He never wanted to be a burden. With a flip of his wrist, he shoved the wheels forward, clearing the small incline of the ramp, and rolled down the pier, until the tip of his front wheels precariously aligned to the edge. Cosmo whined and licked John's hand, then rose and trotted a few feet back up the wood planks to the ramp.

"You're a whiz at reading my moods, Cosmo." John grunted as he peered down at the murky water.

With his head tilted back toward his master, the dog let out two sharp yips. John sucked in a deep breath, exhaled, and forced his attention away from the soul-breaking darkness.

"Thank God for you, you hairy beast." He signaled for the dog to come as he reversed a few feet. "You read my every emotion, don't you, Cosmo?" The German Shepherd plopped his paw on John's leg and whined.

A fish jumped close to the end of the pier, wiggling high into the air, its iridescent scales flashing in the sun before it splashed back into the water. Cosmo's giant ears sprang forward as his tail shifted from a slow wave to a thrashing wag. He pranced in place, his attention fixed on where the shiny thing disappeared into the water.

"Go ahead. I'm staying right here," John said, a smile supplanting the worry lines furrowing his brow.

Cosmo wasted no time and dashed to the edge, barking. After a few woofs, which John was certain meant as a warning to the fish to show himself, he trotted back. John leaned forward to stroke the dog's back and Cosmo shivered but kept his focus on the water for a few seconds before he dutifully shifted his gaze to John, his expressive, caramel eyes transparent with devotion.

"Oh, buddy," John said in a soothing voice. "I'm

okay." He stroked Cosmo's head. "You help lift the burden of my loneliness." With a final pat, he said, "Love you."

Cosmo tilted his head back and forth, then shoved his nose under John's hand, asking for a pet. John willingly stroked the dog as he viewed the afternoon sunlight reflected off the ripples in the water. The thick woods across the lake completed the pastoral scene. John's shoulders relaxed and a sense of peace replaced the earlier angst.

"C'mon, Cosmo." He swung his chair around to head back for shore and the short trip back to his office. "Might as well get this over." With the dog dutifully trotting at his side, he continued the one-sided conversation. "What you ask?" He glanced at Cosmo. "Well, I'll tell you. Before our little hike, while you were chowing down breakfast, I went back to the office and requested a face-to-face with Mariah via Skype. My idea is once she sees me in this chair, she'll run in the opposite direction. Better to yank the band-aid off, right, buddy?"

Secured in his office, John turned on the computer and the ding sounded, indicating new emails. He swung his wheelchair around in time to see the notifications as they downloaded. One was from Mariah. Well, that was fast. His mouth fell open as he silently scanned her answer. In disbelief, he proclaimed to Cosmo, "Yes. Buddy, she said yes."

John finger brushed his hair, *holy moly*, then checked his watch. Thirty minutes away. He rolled backward into the bathroom, and after surveying himself in the mirror, grabbed the hairbrush, and ran a few strategic strokes across his scalp. Next, he ran his tongue along his top row of teeth, inspecting them carefully. Satisfied that no trapped lettuce would sabotage his smile, he gave himself a final once-over and flattened the cotton collar of his polo shirt. Ready or not, here we go.

He counted to ten while Skype connected. Then she appeared. *God, she's beautiful.* And those eyes, so clear blue they're luminescent.

She waved and smiled a warm, friendly smile, then said, "Your profile pictures don't do you justice."

Right. From the chest up. She must know I'm in a wheelchair. It was in my profile.

"Thanks." Before he could continue, Cosmo, his ears forward, plopped his front paws on the desk and peered into the computer screen.

Mariah laughed as Cosmo's head tilted back and forth, apparently intrigued by the talking screen. "Who's the cutie?"

"Cosmo, say hi to the lady." On cue, Cosmo yelped a single bark. John patted his head.

"Good boy." Then, with a quick thrust, he rolled back. Nothing like the impact of a full visual. He sucked in a short breath and waited.

Mariah scooted closer to the screen and squinted. "Is that a Razor Blade all-terrain wheelchair?"

He nodded like a bobble head, unable to speak, despite the fact her gaze remained focused on the chair. *Not the reaction I expected.*

"Trying to read the fine print on the frame, but I'm sure it's a Razor Blade."

A flush of heat swept up his neck and face when she shifted her attention back to him. "Exactly," he said, his voice barely above a whisper.

With a curl at the corners of her mouth, she asked, "Surprised I know about wheelchairs?"

"Surprise would be a good word." He tightened the grip on the wheels of the chair, attempting to clamp down the raw emotion flooding his senses. He swallowed hard to unstick the words caught in his throat. Her calm acceptance of his condition seemed genuine, unlike the feigned acquiescence by other women he'd met.

After a second hard swallow, he said, "Shock would be a better word."

****

Surprised by the hint of cynicism in his response, Mariah said, "My former partner was shot by a drug dealer and ended up paralyzed. I'm his shopping companion when a new model comes out." She leaned back in her chair and rested her interwoven fingers behind her head. "I imagine that model makes it much easier to get around on a horse farm?"

"You don't have a problem with all this?" He gestured downward with a sweep of his hand, indicating his legs.

Before she could answer, the door opened and a stunning, pregnant woman stepped in. Is this guy married? Mariah kept her cool and waved. "Hello."

"Oh, sorry, John." Ariel bent down to screen level, smiled, and returned the wave. "I didn't know you had company." She positioned her hand on her lower back and straightened. "Ugh."

"Mariah, meet my sister, Ariel," he said. A blush bloomed across his face. "She and her husband, Gavin, own the farm."

"Nice to meet you…both," she chuckled. "When

are you due?"

"I'm five months and counting." With a light sweep of her belly, she continued, "This August heat doesn't help but we're excited about a Christmas arrival."

"Well, congratulations. Have you picked out any names?"

"Elmo," John said.

"Enough." Ariel landed a quick thump on John's head. "We know it's a boy, but Gavin and I are still discussing possible names." She raised an eyebrow at John and continued, "Except talks about the name Elmo have ended."

Mariah leaned forward on her desk. "I really like the banter between you two. I'm an only child, so I missed out on the sibling comradery."

"Are your parents still living?" Ariel asked.

"Just my mom." Mariah liked these two, but she struggled to explain her mother's dementia. "She lives nearby." She changed the subject, hoping it wasn't too abrupt.

"How old is Cosmo?"

Ariel made a time-out sign with her hands. "Mariah, before you hear the unedited version of Cosmo, I'm going to say what I hope is a temporary goodbye. Nice chatting with you—" She waved and smiled. "—but I still have rounds to do on the pregnant mares." She squeezed John's shoulder and backed out of view.

"Ready to hear the unabridged version of Cosmo the wonder pup?" John rubbed his dog's head.

Mariah rested her chin in her hands, happy for the escape from work, from her mother's demands, and from her wacky but sweet roommate. John's relaxed attitude made him soothing to be around. It didn't hurt that he was funny and easy on the eyes. "I'm all ears."

Chapter Five

Mariah soaked up the stories of Cosmo's adolescent antics. She particularly relished John's lack of inhibition in relaying his description of chasing Cosmo around the farm in his wheelchair to retrieve one of Ariel's favorite boots. Although the wheelchair confined him physically, it didn't define him mentally. This guy's attitude impressed her, and his sense of humor ranked as good as any stand-up she'd attended. She held her rib cage and heaved a final laugh. "So, you rescued the boot still in one piece?"

John cocked an eye at the alert canine sitting next to him. "Mostly, except for the slobber and a half-chewed finger loop."

"Oh, my." She gazed at her own cordovan-colored leather boots, which she constantly worked on to keep clean and free of scuffs.

Cosmo rested his chin on John's leg. "It's okay, boy." He rubbed the dog's ears before returning his attention to the screen. "My sister is a vet." His head bounced in an overstated nod. "Although murder might have crossed her mind, she took an oath to protect animals."

He glanced down at Cosmo. "Lucky for you, buddy."

The bond between these two struck her as trust, whole and complete. Her chest tightened and an emptiness seized her heart. She lacked that brand of special connection in her life. It struck her as ironic but the kind of relationship she dreamed of, the one that eluded her, screamed from the image on the screen. John's voice snapped her back to the present when he asked her if she'd like to meet in person. *Yes, I would.* She opened her mouth to voice her agreement, but a text alert caught her attention. She glanced at her phone and scanned the message. *Why the heck are they texting me an alert on my cell phone?* She read it again and despite the oddity of a text message, instinct kicked in. "Hey, I gotta go."

"Everything okay?" John asked.

"Nope." Mariah gathered her keys and stood. "Emergency alert for all local wardens to apprehend suspected deer poachers at a nearby nature preserve."

John rocked back and forth in his wheelchair. "I guess you need to go. When do you want to talk again?"

Mariah fumbled as she clipped the keys to her belt before glancing up. "My schedule varies." She brushed the bangs off her flushed face. "I'll email you."

"Okay. I won't hold my breath." He laughed and disconnected the call.

Mariah splayed her hands in exasperation as the screen went blank. "Well, that was kind of abrupt."

A second text alert beeped as she crossed the room to exit. She paused, glancing at the repeated message, and grabbed her radio to respond while flinging open the door. A white piece of folded paper fluttered to the ground. "What now?" Exasperated, she released her thumb from the talk button and stooped to retrieve the note. Holding it by a corner, she shook the folds free and gasped in horror as she read the message, "We're watching you." She dropped the letter as if it burned her fingers. Her head swiveled, and she increased her gait to a jog.

After securing herself in the truck, she peeled out of the parking lot and raced the short distance to the scene. When she arrived at the dimly lit park entrance, it appeared empty. There were no official vehicles. She scanned the lot and spotted a black sedan with dark-tinted windows parked toward the back. An involuntary shiver shook her shoulders as her pickup closed the distance. Her instincts warred between fight and flight. With a shaky hand, she thumbed her microphone button and spoke in a measured tone, "Arrived on scene at Ainsworth Park but no other units here. Where are you guys?"

A voice blared from the speaker, "Say again? No active alert."

She hit the brakes at the same moment a man in a dark hoodie stepped from the rear passenger side door and pointed a rifle in her direction. The sedan's bright lights flared on, blinding her. Dropping the mic, she spun the steering wheel to the right and stepped on the accelerator, sending the truck into a tight U-turn toward the exit. As she fishtailed out of the park, she checked her rear-view mirror and headlights swerved in behind her. She floored the gas pedal. As her gaze darted between the road and mirror, she fished along the side of the console for the microphone cord. *Gotcha.*

With hitched breaths, she held the microphone to her lips. "Request immediate backup on Highway Eighty-Seven, heading West at mile marker fourteen." The landscape zipped by in a dark blur as she continued with her foot heavy on the gas. Both hands gripped the wheel. After what seemed like endless minutes of hurtling down the highway toward backup, she realized there was no reflection of bright headlights in her rear-view. She lost them. Or they quit. Whatever. Relief swamped her, and she released a deep sigh.

As mile marker ten neared, where the law enforcement units waited to intercept her, the adrenaline that raced her pulse and thumped in her chest eased. She floored the gas pedal and switched on her blue and red flashers. *Headed your way, guys.* In a matter of minutes, two separate law enforcement vehicles slid in behind her from the intersection and escorted her the short distance back to headquarters.

As she made the turn into what she'd expected to be an empty parking lot, her jaw dropped at the plethora of law enforcement standing ready behind their car doors in the well-placed spotlights of headquarters. *Are they waiting for me?* She exited her truck and noticed a familiar figure step forward. His face twisted in a stern scowl as he advanced toward her. With his index finger, he motioned her to a spot away from the others.

"What the hell is going on, Officer Michaels?" Frank spoke in a low, restrained tone.

"Am I in trouble 'cause you only call me Officer Michaels when the poopy hits the fan or is about to."

He placed his hands on his hips. "You tell me."

She glanced at the cadre of male officers milling around their cars, projecting a cool demeanor, as they awaited orders from their captain, her captain and a pang of guilt slammed into her chest. All this manpower tied up protecting her from an unknown threat. She dropped her head and stared at the ground.

"I don't know what's going on, sir." She retrieved the note from her pocket and handed it to him. "But it would seem someone has it in for me."

Frank's jaw twitched as he read the note. "I'm keeping this as evidence, and if there's even a smudge of a fingerprint on it, our lab guys will find it."

"Okay." Mariah half-smiled. "I appreciate the help."

The captain rubbed the back of his neck. "Here's what we're going to do. Rather than put you in a safe house which I know you'd resist, I'm sending you out of town. There's a conference in Orlando, Florida that I was going to attend but I'm sending you instead."

"Florida, Captain?"

"Yes, Florida. It's a continuing education symposium in Orlando to get updated on new federal laws and guidelines on the handling of invasive species. You go and gather all the information and share it with the rest of us when you return."

"When do I leave?"

"Tomorrow. Go home and get packed. I'll arrange for the airline ticket and transportation to the airport." He signaled for one of the other officers to join them.

Her mind raced with everything she'd have to do to leave by tomorrow. Should she email John and let him know she'd be in his state? Was it too soon for a face-to-face? Frank's deep voice interrupted her thoughts.

"Tommy here will escort you home. Then, he'll take you to the airport tomorrow. Be ready by eight a.m."

She glanced at Tommy and offered a sheepish nod before turning to Frank. "Got it, boss."

"And, Mariah, stay safe. That's plain English for

stay out of trouble. Don't tell anyone where you're going." Frank faced the officers in the parking lot. "We're good here. Return to your shifts and have an uneventful night." The men dispersed to their units. Without another word, Frank strode to his car and, with a tip of his Stetson as he passed, drove away.

With Tommy hot on her heels, Mariah got into her truck. While she waited for him to pull his car behind hers, she started a mental list of things to do before departure time. John should be at the top of the list. She really liked him and wanted a face-to-face but what kind of crazy would she be to add him to her increasingly chaotic life?

Chapter Six

"Where's the fire?" Tizzy asked Mariah as clothes flew over her head into an open suitcase.

"Last minute travel for work." Tapping her index finger against her lips, Mariah glanced around the room. "What am I forgetting?"

Tizzy peered into the medium-sized luggage. "Underwear, t-shirts, jeans, tennis shoes…check. Cowgirl boots? Where are you headed?"

Frank's final instruction was to tell no one where I was going. That would include my roommate, but she'll pester me until I tell her something. She checked her watch. *And I have thirty minutes of potential pestering before Tommy picks me up.* "Out of town."

"Why?"

"To attend a conference for my boss." Mariah continued loading her suitcase with intentional nonchalance, thankful Tizzy didn't pick up on the misdirection.

"Why so last minute?"

Mariah struggled for the right answer. *If these thugs find my apartment and Tizzy isn't alerted to a potential threat and something happens to her…. On the other hand, the word dizzy rhymes appropriately with Tizzy. If questioned, her response will read like an article from Confession magazine.* "Something came up and my boss can't go." *I'm not a total liar.*

"Does your mom know where you're going?"

"No. You know how my mother worries about me flying." Mariah fiddled with strands of pearls before stuffing them into a velvet jewelry bag.

"Oh, I see. So, you're not telling her you're leaving?"

"No, I'll tell her once I've landed." Mariah noticed a scowl on Tizzy's face and added, "I'll FaceTime with her at night."

"I'm available to help her if anything comes up." Tizzy's face relaxed into a smile.

Tizzy helping her absent-minded parent had big mess written all over it, so rather than agree, she hugged her roommate and said, "Thanks. That's sweet of you to offer but her neighbor, Franny, is next door if anything comes up."

Tizzy splayed her hands and shrugged her shoulders. "You're telling her neighbor about your trip and your mother once you land but you won't share the details with me?"

"Actually, I haven't said anything to Franny yet. I figured it wasn't necessary unless my mom called me for help."

"I give up. Keep your secrets," Tizzy said, her shoulders slumped as she stepped to the bedroom door and stopped. "Have a great trip." She exited with a back-handed wave over her shoulder.

Ugh. I can't leave like this. "Tizzy. Wait. We need to talk." Mariah tossed the last few items in her suitcase, then zipped and locked the top. She gathered her jacket and slung her purse over her shoulder. After a quick glance around her room and satisfied she hadn't left anything behind, she tipped the suitcase onto its wheels, when a door slammed. Curious, she jerked the suitcase into motion and entered an empty living room.

"Tizzy?" She leaned back to view her roommate's bedroom. *Her door's open but the room is dark.* A shudder assailed her body. She tamped down the unease and rationalized her reaction as nerves from last night's bizarre events, but when her phone chimed, she started. "Enough!"

With a deep breath, she retrieved her phone from her purse. *Tommy. Thank goodness. I'm so ready to bail.*

****

As her plane approached the runway into the Orlando airport, Mariah gazed raptly at her destination. Different in so many ways from her normal locale, she welcomed the change. Relief washed through her. She leaned back in her window seat. In a matter of hours, she'd be relaxing by the hotel pool, a glass of wine in her hand, poring over the conference itinerary. She arranged a few extra days after the meeting for a road trip to Ocala, just in case. An image of John flashed through her mind as the wheels bounced on the tarmac. A smile bloomed across her face. *Oh, my gosh. I'm here, in Florida.* The illuminated seatbelt light turned off and the exit scramble started.

"Your huge grin tells me you're happy to be in the Sunshine state," the flight attendant said with a practiced smile as she stood at the exit door. "Business or pleasure?"

"Both…I hope." Mariah hesitated in the doorway while she slid her purse over her shoulder and looped the cumbersome carry-on's strap over her head for better control. With a quick nod and thanks, she depaned.

"Have a good trip," the woman called after her.

"That's the plan," she muttered as she shuffled in unison with the crowd toward baggage claim and the rental car counters. The aroma of fried food wafted across her nose. She ignored the urge to beeline into the closest restaurant despite a growl of protest from her stomach. Instead, she turned on her cell phone as she walked. Within seconds, a series of dings signaled the download of successive calls and texts. *I knew it. Okay.* She peered at the phone screen. *Who needs me the most?*

One message caught her eye. Tizzy asked if she'd arrived at her secret location yet. Annoyed at the unspoken but obvious snide tone that accompanied the words, Mariah texted back, *—Yes, in Omaha, Nebraska.—* Let her chew on that for a while. With a quick perusal of the list of callers and relief her mother wasn't one of them, she stuffed her phone in her back pocket.

After getting her rental car, she entered the hotel's address into her GPS and exhaled a long, deep breath. Stress peeled off her psyche like dried skin off a sunburned back. Time slowed as she drove at an easy pace to the resort. She had all afternoon to catch up on the backlog of calls, eat, whatever. *God, I can't believe I have an afternoon of whatever, like a hot bath and a glass of white wine.*

After checking into her room and gloating over the upgrade the clerk volunteered, Mariah tugged her phone from her back pocket, with the same reluctance she would change a dirty diaper and flopped onto the bed.

She rolled her eyes and spoke to the textured

ceiling. "Might as well get this out of the way."

Her first text was to her boss. —*Arrived without incident. Tucked away in luxury hotel room. Love da perks of this job. LOL.*—

He responded with an immediate reply. —*Glad. Pick a safe word. Use if trouble.*—

—*Really?*—

—*Yeah, really.*—

Mariah decided to continue the joke. —*Omaha, Nebraska.*—

—*That's two words, smart-ass.*—

She giggled as she typed. —*I can count.*—

—*Officer Michaels. Be vigilant.*—

—*Always am, boss.*—

He ended with a thumb's up emoji.

Mariah scrolled to the next entry and her heart quickened as the name John Armstrong appeared. The one worded text read, —*Email?*—

Oh crap. I forgot to email him about my schedule. What time did he send it? *Ouch.* Early this morning while she was in the air on her way to Florida.

She texted back. —*Sorry, forgot. Talk?*—

She rolled on her side and stared at the phone dial for a full minute but a deep growl from her stomach reminded her of the last time she ate, no, gobbled a cup of yogurt. *Predawn. Too long.* The restaurant bragged of three on-site places to eat. With her service weapon secured in her shoulder bag and her phone stuffed in her back pocket, she made her way to the lobby.

A blast of humid air hit her body as the automatic doors opened, allowing a cadre of male game wardens to enter together. Dressed in matching green fatigues, identifying insignia and work boots, they couldn't have been more obvious or rowdy. Neither was the way they gawked at her, with one of them offering a low whistle as he passed, while a second male, in a guttural tone, commented, "Hey, beautiful."

She glanced at her own casual attire of t-shirt, jeans, and tennis shoes. An unease accosted her self-confidence, and she straightened the hem of her cotton top. The uniform equalized the work environment and minimized overt flirting.

They arrived simultaneously at the hostess stand. One of the males, in a not-so-subtle leer, leaned forward and asked, "Are you free tonight? Drinks in the hotel bar?"

Great. Borderline creepy. I wish I had my badge. One flash of that shiny metal object would end this.

"Sorry, man." She half-smiled. "Got to get my beauty sleep for the conference on invasive species tomorrow."

She added, "You know, the one hosted by the Florida Wildlife Commission." *Wait for it.* After a few seconds. *Bam!* Glances between the men swerved like a driver on an icy freeway.

'Mr. Hey Beautiful.' talked first. "You're a game warden?" His eyes swept her body.

"Yes. A *Texas* game warden," she said, with an emphasis on Texas.

"Miss, your table is ready." The hostess tucked a large menu under her arm and strolled into the dining room.

Without a backward glance, Mariah followed the woman to a table for two in the corner. She faced a plate glass window with an outside view and didn't see 'Mr. Hey Beautiful' approach until he slid into the seat opposite her.

"Truce?" He held his hands in the air.

"Depends." She crossed her arms and tapped her bicep.

"I wanted to properly introduce myself." He stuck out his right hand. "I'm Chad."

She clasped it with a hearty grip. "I'm Mariah Michaels from Fort Worth."

"Hi, Mariah. Nice to meet you. There's room at our table. Want to join us for lunch?"

She glanced at the table of fresh-faced, stud wannabes, all grins, and head nods in her direction. "Sure." *Wait until Frank hears about my interagency fraternizing.* When they arrived at the table, Chad slid out the one empty chair and waited until she was seated before he made introductions.

"Quite the gentleman," she said, gazing up at him through her eyelashes.

"I have my moments," he replied, shooting a don't-you-dare glare toward the other men.

After trading war stories about dealing with drunk boaters, poachers and unlicensed hunters, Mariah directed the conversation to invasive species in Florida and specifically the Burmese Python. "How many Burmese pythons do you think inhabit the Everglades?"

"Hard to tell," Chad said. "They're stealthy predators. The numbers I have indicate captures. For example, in the two breeding seasons, nearly two hundred adult pythons, including female pythons, carrying more than four thousand developing eggs have been removed."

"Hmm." Mariah drummed her fingers on the table. "Devastating outcome if not controlled."

Chad nodded and continued, "The goal is to implant radio transmitters onto male "scout snakes" which can then lead biologists to reproductively active female pythons, which can then be euthanized."

The waitress, overhearing the last part of Chad's answer, laid Mariah's plate in front of her and said, "This conversation is not for the faint of heart."

Mariah and Chad exchanged knowing glances before Mariah replied, "Our job as law enforcement officers does carry risk but so does yours."

Responding to the bewildered expression on the waitress's face, Mariah offered a two-word explanation, "'Hangry' customers." She scooped her fork full of tuna. "Never underestimate the outrage from the lunch construction crew who ate a boiled egg for breakfast. Or the ones who can't enjoy their dining experience if they haven't sent their food back at least once." She slid the fork in her mouth. "Mmm. This is delicious."

The waitress responded with a brief laugh. "You've got that right and glad you like the tuna salad." She surveyed the group at the table. "Anyone need anything?"

Mariah and Chad shook their heads in simultaneous response while the rest of the team shoveled food in silent consent. For the next hour, Mariah enjoyed the disjointed conversation that ensued. What interested her the most was hearing about the different challenges that Florida Game Wardens faced versus her own experiences. A sense of camaraderie prevailed, and the guys treated her as one of their own.

With the last satisfying bite, Mariah put her fork down and patted her stomach. "I needed that." Her phone buzzed and she gasped at the number on the screen. John. Calling her back. Now.

Mariah peered up at the faces studying her. *Oh boy.* She had to answer or risk John thinking she was avoiding him. After positioning her earpiece, she tapped the answer icon. His boyish face appeared. *Of all times to Skype.*

"Hi there," she said, tucking her hair behind her ear, trying her absolute hardest to be casual. "I'm sorry I didn't send my schedule. I meant to."

"I believe you." John smiled. "I hear noise. Are you at a meeting?"

"No, lunch in a busy restaurant." Chad leaned over and waved into the phone. Mariah swatted at his hand and murmured, "Go away."

"Is now not a good time?" John said, his brow furrowed.

Mariah positioned her face closer and focused all her attention on the screen. "Now's fine. That guy is a colleague."

"Are they all colleagues?" John pointed behind Mariah's head.

She whipped around and two of the guys were flashing the sign for surf's up, the other two were offering the peace sign. "Guys, this is not a group chat. Behave or be gone." The men jabbed each other and laughed on their way back to their seats. She faced John and said, "they are all game wardens. I'm at a conference on invasive species."

"Oh, I don't remember you mentioning an upcoming conference the last time we talked." John folded his arms and narrowed his eyes.

"I know." Mariah, realizing the tone of the conversation was going South, used her free hand to dig out a twenty, which she slapped on the table. After a nod goodbye to her table mates, she hurried out of the restaurant and scanned the area for a more private place to talk. "My boss was scheduled to attend but put me in as his replacement. It was very last minute." *Should I spill the beans now?*

"Where's the conference being held?"

Beans are gonna be spilled in three, two, one. "Orlando, Florida." The answer came out as a squeak, so she repeated, "Orlando, Florida."

"That explains why the uniform you wore the other day is different from the photobombing dudes, but it doesn't explain why you didn't tell me you're in Florida."

"Long story." Mariah sighed. "But I want to read you in."

"I see." John waved to someone entering his office and then continued. "Look. I get it. You're busy. I gotta go but we can talk another time."

"I don't mind telling you how I ended up being sent to Florida on short notice." She glanced around and hesitated. "I'd just rather do it in person."

"Text me when you're free."

"How 'bout I send you the schedule I promised?"

"I'll be waiting." He disconnected the call.

****

"Was that Mariah?" Ariel asked.

"Yeah." John drummed his fingers on the arm of his wheelchair, keeping his gaze on his lap.

"You don't sound enthused. What happened?"

"She's in Orlando but didn't bother sharing the intel that she'd be in Florida for a conference."

"Orlando?" Ariel squealed. "For how long? Can

she drive here and meet us?"

"Sis, did you hear what I said?" John snapped.

"My hearing is fine, *bro*. Call her back and invite her up for dinner."

"Don't you think if she was interested in a live meet-up, she'd have let me know her plan to come to Florida?" He raked his fingers through his hair then flopped his hands onto his lap.

"She was probably scrambling to get out the door, busy with last minute details. Don't over think it."

He whistled. "Sis, that's a lot of 'womansplaining.' A text would have been nice."

Ariel grabbed her brother's face. "Who could possibly not fall in love with this mug? Hmm?"

John swatted her hand away. "Then again…." He trailed off, sweeping his hand over his paralyzed lower body.

"This one is special, and she likes you. I feel it in my preggo gut."

"I'm going for a stroll," John said, as he backed his wheelchair from under the desk.

Ariel blocked his movement. "I want to meet Mariah. I'll invite her if you don't."

John raised his arms in surrender. "I'm dialing, I'm dialing."

Chapter Seven

Mariah tugged her suitcase through the hotel lobby toward the exit while scanning a text from Chad. He flirted like a pro with her the entire convention and made his interest sunshine clear.

The current message read, *—Join me for an adventure to Sea World? I promise we'll have fun.—*

She had to hand it to him. He was persistent. Pausing on the front porch, she typed her response,*—Thanks for the invite but I'm headed to Ocala to visit friends.—* She paused and at the risk of sending the wrong message, she added*, —Another time.—*

Their comradery transformed what would have been solitary mealtimes and lonely nights into drinking dart games at the bar. Chad killed karaoke night. The man sang country like a Texas cowboy. She liked him and hoped they could continue their friendship, but he didn't make her heart race the way John did. Her phone pinged.

—By any chance does the guy on the phone live in Ocala?—

—Yes.—

—I hope it works out. Stay in touch.—

—Still friends?—

—Of course. I'm here if you need anything. Safe travels.—

—TKU.— Mariah tapped the back arrow and

closed the text window, putting the conference in her rear-view.

Happy she'd sent John her schedule as promised, he'd responded with a phone call and an invitation to visit the farm…where she'd meet the family. Yikes!

Mariah hurried to her rental car. Aware she still had a two-hour drive before landing at the farm, she tossed her things in the back seat and whipped out of the parking lot with a screech of tires. John texted her the address and additional directions earlier that morning since, as he put it, they lived 'on a long and winding road.' *I like a clever guy, and this one comes with musical references.*

The Florida Turnpike loomed ahead. Her stomach churned with trepidation as she zipped up the on-ramp. She faced challenges and uncertainty every day in her job, with danger recently added to the mix, but this involved her heart, a far scarier scenario. What was she walking into? Not a normal date. Because John lived with his family, she assumed they were very protective. The sister seemed nice but what about the husband? The housekeeper? The dog?

Contemplation about the visit distracted her past the yellow merge sign onto I-75 until the large green exit sign to Ocala popped into view. With a quick shift to the right, she drove down the ramp and turned left. She fitted her ear bud and dialed John to let him know she was headed down the aforementioned 'long and winding road'. Anticipation fluttered in her chest. The phone rang four times and went to voice mail. *Not a good sign.* A concentrated flow of doubt stormed her self-confidence like the march of army ants. *Maybe I should check into a hotel and fly back tomorrow. Can I honestly handle more uncertainty in my life right now?*

Mariah scanned ahead as she drove. Truck stops, fast-food restaurants and by-the-hour motels lined the roadside, but the availability of popular brand hotels appeared nonexistent. When she'd traveled on her own, without a government expense account, she'd stayed in sketchy, cheap motels, but only after insisting the front desk provided a fresh change of sheets. She heaved a deep sigh. Today, she wasn't in the mood. She'd press on. Literally. Her foot stomped on the gas pedal and the car shot forward. After a few minutes, the congestion surrounding the interstate disappeared and a lush, pastoral landscape, with a relaxing vibe rose from the horizon. She leaned forward, peering over the steering wheel at the rustic beauty painting both sides of the road. Her foot lifted off the throttle—intermittent oohs and aahs tumbled from her lips.

The two-lane road wound in lazy s-curves through acres of farmland designated for the sole purpose of breeding high-quality horseflesh. Originally cut from a live oak forest, random old trees dotted the lush, emerald pastures. Horses, protected by white rail fences, their tails swishing flies away, grazed in peaceful luxury accompanied by an occasional goat or burro companion. Time slowed. She eased her foot off the gas and rolled down the window. She freed her long, thick hair from the purple scrunchie which usually held it hostage in a ponytail and tossed her head. The breeze whipped the loose strands around her face as the radio blared a country tune. Relaxed more than she's been in weeks, she tapped the steering wheel in unison to the popular beat. If it's meant to be….

****

"Have you heard from Mariah?" Ariel clapped her hands together. "It's getting late."

"Sis, your excitement for the arrival of *my* guest is endearing," he said with a tinge of sarcasm. "Long hours working the farm doesn't leave you much opportunity for girl time. I get it. You're lonely." He mimicked playing a violin.

"Zip it, you little Elmo freak." Ariel laughed. "Aren't you the least bit nervous?"

"Not the slightest." He glanced at his phone. "Oh, my freaking god." He fumbled the phone, which hit the floor with a bounce. "I missed a call from Mariah."

"Sure, not an itsy bit nervous there, tiger?" Ariel imitated the crying emoji. "Well, hurry up. Call her back." Ariel picked up the phone and handed it to John. "She's probably on the side of the road, lost, cussing your slack ass."

"Stop enjoying my trepidation so much," he said with a smirk as he hit redial.

"Hi. Where are you?" His head jerked up and he silently mimed to his sister, "She's at the front entrance." His voice squeaked. "I'm glad you're here." He cleared his throat. "I'll open the gate. Drive forward to the circular drive and I'll meet you in front of the house…Yeah. See you soon."

John punched the off button, stuffed the phone in the chair's side pouch and announced to his sister, "She's here, right now, out front." His anxiety climbed as the reality they'd be face to face in a matter of minutes punched him in the gut. It was one thing to flirt from the safety of his home office and be viewed from the waist up but quite another to attempt it from a permanent sitting position. He pounded his lifeless thighs and yelled, "Move, you worthless bastards."

Ariel grabbed his fists. "You're fine, bro. She knows you ride a chair." With a soft stroke to his cheek, she added, "Be your winning self. I'll find Gavin and meet you out front." She blew him a kiss and exited with a back-handed wave.

The outer screen door closed with a bang. John flinched, then combed his fingers through his thick brown hair. With a final glance in the mirror, he nodded at his choice of a grey plaid shirt and called Cosmo. "You got my six?" he asked.

Cosmo barked twice. "Good boy." He inhaled a deep breath. "Let's do this."

John rounded the edge of the front driveway in time to catch a glimpse of Mariah swinging her long, muscular legs from the car. Shorts. She wore tight denim shorts. With his heart throbbing in his throat, he waved and rolled up next to her. "Welcome." Heat flushed his neck as she bent down for a hug. "Need help with your luggage?"

"No, I only have an overnight bag to carry in." She spun in a half circle. "Wow. This place is stunning."

Gavin and Ariel strolled up and Ariel added, "We love farm life. Hi, Mariah, so nice to meet you in person." Ariel embraced Mariah and then stepped back to put her arm around Gavin's waist. "This is my husband, Gavin."

Mariah stuck out her hand and Gavin grabbed her palm in his typical vice hold. Amused, John waited for Mariah to call uncle, but she gave as good as she got. A smile crept across Gavin's face. He let go. "Welcome."

****

Gavin's knuckle-cracking handshake accompanied

by a glacial gaze from his pale blue eyes served as a test. Mariah understood his wariness, but what could she say to assuage his concern? Nothing, really. She wanted to explore possibilities with John. No other agenda. "Thanks, Gavin. You have a beautiful property and so well kept." She turned her attention to John with a huge grin. "Great directions."

Before John could comment, Gavin interjected, "He's a computer whiz. One of his many talents." He nodded toward John. "Why don't you show Mariah your office while Ariel and I check on lunch preparations." Gavin addressed Mariah with a wink. "It's quite a setup."

"She'd probably find my computers and security screens boring, Gav."

"Not at all, John, but I'd love to see the horses while there's still daylight."

"Oh, are you a horse lover too?" John's face lit up.

"I'm an animal lover. It's one of the reasons I became a game warden, but I find horses both majestic and intuitive. They're in my top five of favorite animals."

Ariel punched Gavin's arm as if to dispute his barely veiled suspicions of their guest. She tilted her head toward Mariah. "She's my new best friend."

Mariah belly-laughed and embraced Ariel in a warm hug. "I'm all in."

"Okay, break it up, you two." John laughed. Then waved his arm in an 'after you' gesture.

Cosmo spun in circles around Mariah and barked as if to say, "I'm all in too."

As Gavin and Ariel sauntered toward the house, Gavin snugged Ariel close to his side, rubbing her belly as they walked. She responded by encircling her arm around his waist. Mariah's chest tightened and her heart ached. She'd never seen her parents show that level of affection. In her estimation, the fault lay squarely on her father's shoulders. He lacked empathy and held unachievable expectations. She wondered how they'd been intimate enough to conceive her.

Cosmo bumped her hand with his nose, interrupting her dismal thoughts. His head tilted upward while his soulful amber eyes focused on her face.

"You want a scratch, buddy?"

He answered with a yip, then squatted in a perfect sit. "Oh, you're so easy to read." While a smile claimed her face, she rubbed his ears, then his head, and finished with long, soft belly strokes.

"You're gonna spoil him," John teased. "Cosmo, forward."

Without hesitation, the German Shepherd leapt to attention and fell in place next to John, poised to lead the way as soon as the chair wheels shifted.

Heat surged up Mariah's neck. "I forgot he's a service dog." She touched John's shoulder. "Am I even supposed to pet him?"

"Only when he's not working, but with my disability, he's on duty twenty-four seven."

Mariah gripped her bottom lip in her teeth. "John, I'm so sorry."

John's face exhibited an unnatural tranquility. "Actually, you paid me the best possible compliment by petting my service dog."

"Huh?" Mariah's embarrassment raked her self-confidence raw. *Is he screwing with me?* She attempted to speak but the words felt like stones in her throat.

Clearing her throat didn't help.

John's hazel eyes glimmered as a broad smile spread across his face. "You forgot I was handicapped." His voice husked. "Thank you."

"You're welcome." Puzzled by his comment, she asked, "Have other people, well, women, been put off by your situation?"

"Yes, and they ran for the exit. But others acted the opposite. They viewed me as a meal ticket, or a meal on wheels." He chuckled at his own joke. "One view of this estate and they think they'll hook up with me and win the lottery. Then, they find out I don't own this property and they're out of here faster than a bottle rocket."

Mariah knelt in front of him and put her hands on his knees. Tears burned her eyes. She swallowed over a suffocating lump in her throat. "Is that what you thought?" Worry etched across her face. "God, John. That's not me. No way would I use you or anyone for money." She shook her head, then continued, "But I guess trust is earned."

John motioned for her to lean in and when she complied, he touched his forehead against hers. An errant tear rolled down her cheek and dropped on her hand. Cosmo plopped his paw on top of her hand and perked his ears forward.

She wrapped one arm around Cosmo's neck. "What a special dog you are."

His lips curled back, letting his tongue loll out. He tilted his head to the side as if he understood her compliment and the emotion between them.

"It's just you're so beautiful." John held her gaze.

"Well, thank you. From what I can tell, you're a

spectacular human being."

"Where do we go from here?" John asked.

Ariel called out, "Hey, you two. Lunch is served."

She laughed. "I reckon we're going to lunch.

Chapter Eight

"What a spread," Mariah said as she peered at the banquet-sized, oak table jam-packed with fresh farm veggies, ham slices, and every other yummy edible.

Ariel indicated Mariah's seat was next to John's and across from her and Gavin. The fresh-from-the-oven smell of biscuits, the kind her mother used to bake for special occasions, wafted into the room and up her nose as a plump, elderly woman bustled in carrying a napkin-covered basket. The woman had a welcoming smile and a busy demeanor as she placed the basket in the center of the table. "Hello." Mariah nodded at her.

"This is Bessie Mae, our housekeeper, den mother and—"

"The boss," Gavin finished as he shot a sly smile at the older woman.

"I see." Mariah grinned her approval. "Nice to meet you, boss."

"Tsk, tsk. He only refers to me with that moniker because I know where all the bodies are buried." Ariel placed her hands on her hips and raised an eyebrow at him.

"Oh, that's a story I want to hear." Mariah rubbed her hands together.

Gavin grunted. "Not good dinner conversation."

"More like a fireside chat with lots of alcohol," John added.

"Even better," Mariah said, then threw her head back, laughing. She caught a glimpse of Bessie Mae, her face alight with joy, as she scanned the individuals seated at the table. Despite no blood relation, these were her people.

Bessie Mae dusted her hands on her apron. "Anyone need anything before I go?"

"Join us," Gavin encouraged.

"Thanks, but I have my Zoom book club meeting in ten minutes."

Gavin and John exchanged surprised glances. "You use Zoom?" asked Gavin.

"You have a computer?" asked John.

"Now, children," Bessie Mae playfully chided before she sashayed through the portal and disappeared.

"She's quite a character," Mariah commented.

"Some would say, a one-man army," Ariel said with a chuckle.

"Some would say, indeed, my beautiful wife." Gavin leaned over and kissed Ariel on her rosy cheek. "Chow's getting cold. Let's eat."

Mariah couldn't help but notice Ariel glowed, a result of all the pregnancy hormones. "I have to agree with you, Gavin. Ariel is absolutely radiant."

"Yeah, it's distracting," he said in a low growl, his desire-filled gaze fixed on her face.

"Easy, man. You're going to set the table on fire." John winked at Ariel, who faked embarrassment and fanned her face.

Could it get any better? Could these people be any more welcoming and easier to be around? She'd kept her expectations low out of self-preservation. Between managing her mother's creeping dementia, the demands of her profession, and now a stalker grabbing most of her attention, the idea of adding the complexities of a long-distance relationship overwhelmed her.

John tapped her arm, then handed her a bowl of steamed corn. He leaned in and whispered, "You okay?"

She responded with a nod and in a teasing whisper replied, "Yes." The scent of musk, mixed with fresh wood shavings filled her nose and rocked her senses. Could he smell any sexier?

He touched her hand, and a warm wave swept her stomach. A man more concerned about her than himself. A true anomaly, at least in her experience. An intimacy she enjoyed with him, with Ariel, with everything about this place, so pleasurable, so intense, it approximated an orgasm.

****

John observed the way Mariah fit right into his family dynamic. Bright, mentally quick, and engaged, she accepted their relentless banter and occasional sarcasm. When the conversation turned to her life in Texas, she revealed her mother's dementia. She framed what must be a crushing source of worry, in a matter-of-fact way, without sounding like a victim or casting her mother as a burden. Although surprised she hadn't told him about it during one of their previous calls, he understood how difficult discussing a debilitating condition slowly eating away her mother's memory might be. He also better understood her apparent preoccupation during dinner. Certain she was mulling over how they'd negotiate a long-distance relationship and with him in a wheelchair.... He'd convince her it was possible. Bottom line.

After dinner, and she'd persuaded Ariel to let her help with the cleanup, they headed back to the cottage. Once inside, she braced her arms on his legs and leaned in for a kiss.

"That was out of the blue," John said, touching his lips.

"Thanks for inviting me here." She stood and ran her hands down her pants legs. "I didn't realize how much I needed a change of scenery. And your family. Just wow."

"They are pretty great." John pursed his lips, then cleared his throat. "Listen, Mariah, we need to talk."

"Uh-oh, what?"

"I need to get something off my chest."

"I'm listening." She tilted her head.

"I can't dance." Staring down at his legs, he shrugged, holding his palms up.

Mariah clasped her arms behind her back and, with a pensive gaze, peered up at the ceiling for a full minute. John held his breath waiting for her to speak.

"Can you gaze upon the stars twinkling in the night?" Her index finger aimed toward the window. "Can you feel the wind brush against your cheek?" She twirled her hand in the air. "Can you inhale the fragrance of newly mowed hay?"

His throat tightened and he swallowed hard. "Yes."

"Then you can dance."

"You say that now but what happens when I can't do something you want."

"Like what?"

"How about surfing?"

"Surfing?" She guffawed. "I don't surf."

He rolled his eyes. "The point is, I don't want to

hold you back. You're active and outdoorsy."

She strolled to his solid oak front door and peeked out the eye-level decorative glass pane, then flung it wide open. "Take a look, John." She waved her hand, indicating the acres of rolling hills. "And you're not?"

Hope swelled as he flamed out in his attempts to sway her against a relationship with him. He admired the effort she was investing. She clearly wanted this. His fear of rejection diminished, ebbing like a low tide. "I can see I won't win this battle."

Mariah heaved a huge sigh. "Finally." She smiled. "Let's see where this takes us."

John patted his lap and indicated for her to sit. She sat crosswise on his lap and flung her arm around his neck, fondling the fine hair along his neckline. His heart pounded against his chest as she stroked up and down. He clutched her face with both hands, gliding his thumb over her cheek. She licked her full lips and closed the distance to his mouth. He tasted the after-dinner coffee on her tongue, breathed in her floral scent, and allowed the kiss to assault his senses. She moaned as his tongue danced with hers, exploring the warm corners.

Breathless, he leaned back. "Stay with me," he whispered, "with us," —he nodded toward Cosmo— "tonight rather than the main house."

With her eyebrow raised, Mariah flashed a devilish grin. "Let's see what you got, Marine." One-handed, she yanked up his t-shirt. "Ooh, nice." She traced the red Semper Fi motto, tattooed in a semicircle across his left pectoral muscle.

His upper body shuddered as she sprinkled light kisses over his nipples and morphed him into a mindless mess. Heck, her mere closeness sent him into orbit. He wanted to return the favor. His hands closed over hers, directing them, along with the top, over his head. Bare-chested, he grasped her blouse, but she slapped his hand away.

"I'm not done admiring your tattoos, mister," she said with sass. "What's with this mean-mugged bulldog tattoo on your arm?"

"That's Chesty, the Marine Corp mascot…now official…." His mouth gaped open. Mum, as she slowly and deliberately unbuttoned her shirt.

"Charming," she said, never leaving his gaze.

"What the hell, woman?" he asked, already shifting the wheels of his chair toward the bedroom door.

"What took you so long?" she said, her voice husky with desire.

****

The next morning, Mariah awoke to a soft tap on the front door of the cottage. John slept soundly beside her.

Naked, she sprinted out of bed, tossed one of John's t-shirts over her head and stepped into her blue jeans one leg at a time, hobbling toward the door and the second, louder knock.

She opened the shade. Ariel stood on the front porch holding a large, hammered silver tray with a full complement of coffee, eggs, and toast. She smiled and held the tray out as an offering. Mariah twisted the door handle, certain a flowering blush covered her face, and waved her in. "Good morning. You didn't have to fetch us breakfast."

"I was coming over anyway to assist John with his morning routine." Ariel ambled into the kitchen and set down the tray before turning to Mariah, her shoulders squared. "How much do you know about spinal cord injuries?"

"A little. My former partner suffered a spinal cord injury after a job-related gunshot. He was single without a family close by, so I volunteered as his initial caregiver while other arrangements were made. I accompanied him to all the doctor's appointments, rehab sessions and physical therapy classes."

"I'm impressed," Ariel said, relaxing her stance. "So, you *are* aware of the morning routine?"

"Generally, yes."

"My brother's progress is way ahead of schedule, but I still help him, despite his objections."

"John hasn't said much about his life prior to the accident. A bit of history would help me understand everything he's been through and how I can best assist him."

Ariel clasped Mariah's hand. "That's a lovely gesture and I agree but you didn't hear it from me." She ducked her head. "John is a very humble guy."

Mariah ran her index finger and thumb along her lips. "Mum's the word."

"John was destined for success. He thrived on winning. After graduating from college as the senior class valedictorian, he joined the Marines to follow in his father's footsteps."

"Oh, your father was in the military?"

Ariel pointed to an eight-by-ten framed picture of a handsome young man in a Marine uniform on the bookshelf in the kitchen. "Our father was the ultimate hero. A man who gave his life serving his country. John was still in our mother's womb when a nineteen-ton truck loaded with massive amounts of explosives crashed into the Marine barracks in Beirut, Lebanon. Two hundred forty service members died that day, including our father." Her breath hitched. "All that remained were a few grainy pictures and his singed dog tags recovered from the rubble, which I wore until Gavin replaced the sad memory with a diamond pendent."

"Your poor mother, having to raise you two all alone."

Ariel pressed her lips together and swiped at a tear. "We tried to steer him away from joining the military, but duty to serve flowed through his blood. He was driven, although what drove him wasn't clear. Was it purpose to fulfill dad's legacy or perhaps exact revenge on the terrorists responsible for transforming our mother into an overworked widow with the challenge of raising two fatherless children? Either way, he couldn't wait to get into the fight and completed Officer Candidate School in record time. With the rank of second lieutenant and the responsibility of a platoon of men, he was dropped into a hot zone. The outcome is obvious."

"What's going on?" John asked as he rolled into the kitchen, concern clear on his face.

"Your sister was just filling me in on the schedule." Mariah kept her voice even. "Would you like me to stay or go?"

Without answering her directly, he said, "I could use your help with Cosmo. He needs his morning constitution *too*. Would you mind?"

Mariah sensed John's discomfort but caught his reference to both needing a constitution. "Not at all.

Here, Cosmo," she said, without missing a beat.

Cosmo, keen for John's okay, waited until his master waved his hand, then trotted out the open door and sat at attention.

"Good boy." John patted his heart.

Mariah blew John a kiss as she backed up toward the door. "Don't worry. I've got this."

John nodded and smiled. "No doubt." He bowed his head for two seconds, then said, "I'd like you to stay a few more days if possible."

"I'll call Frank on the walk and ask for two extra days."

"I like a woman who doesn't hesitate. Breakfast when you get back?" he asked.

"Check." She raced after Cosmo, who twirled in impatient circles at the bottom of the stairs.

****

"I take it things are going rather well with Mariah," Ariel said.

"Why do I get the idea that's more of a question than a statement." John squinted his eyes.

"Hey, it's all good. I really like her."

"Then stop giving her the third degree." He crossed his arms.

"Whoa, little brother. I need to know she's fully aware of—"

He cut her off and seethed. "Aware of what? Say it."

Ariel stuttered, then ran her hands through her hair and lowered her head, cheeks flushed.

"Aware of my limitations?" He fisted his hands. "Aware of what I can't do? Aware I'm not whole?" Through gritted teeth, he continued, "Look at me."

Silence draped like a heavy curtain. After several agonizing minutes, Ariel raised her head. Tears streamed down her face and her chest heaved.

John beckoned Ariel to him and drew her into a tight embrace. "I appreciate everything you and Gavin have done for me," he muttered, "but give me a little credit. I've built my own company. I support myself." After a gentle squeeze, he released his hold.

"I know and I only want what's best for you." She choked out the words as she took a step back.

"She's what's best for me."

"I don't doubt that for a minute, but we're in an ideal situation here on the farm. What happens when you relocate to Texas and she's working long hours out in the field and you need help, like this morning, with your bowel program?"

"I honestly don't know." He shook his head as he answered. "I do know I want this time with her."

"No judgement, but I'm fairly certain you two slept together last night and achieved a certain level of intimacy?"

"We did but helping me achieve a bowel movement requires a deeper and different level of intimacy, one I'm not ready to share with her yet."

"I get it." Ariel inhaled a deep breath and blew it out. "I really do. And I'm certain you'll handle it." She waved her hand toward the bathroom. "So, let's take care of business before she gets back."

****

Mariah relished the hours she spent with John roaming the farm's vast pastures in a specially outfitted ATV. He was uber easy to talk to and they covered a plethora of subjects. Most guys she dated talked about themselves, extolling their accomplishments, none of which could be verified, until she mentally drifted off into Lalaland. But John asked her questions about her childhood, her career, and her family with genuine interest.

They finished the day with a swim in the Olympic-sized pool. Cosmo swam alongside John with what he referred to as a smiley face. In the evening, the family gathered around a fire pit and roasted hot dogs and marshmallows. Gavin related the humorous side of being a SEAL. The name stood for Sea, Air and Land but after the hilarity of the stories, a more accurate name, in her view at least, would be Sea, Air and Laughs.

After dinner, John asked Mariah to come to his office with him.

"Very impressive," she said as she viewed an assortment of hi-tech computers, monitors, and stacked metal boxes she didn't recognize. "I had no idea."

"I did tell you I run a security business, correct?"

"Yeah, but I didn't know you do such high-level intelligence work." She thumbed the binders on one of the shelves and read the titles aloud, "Homeland Security, FBI, Alachua County Sheriff's Department, and the list goes on."

John wore a mischievous grin as he beckoned her to come sit on his lap. "I operate with a top-secret clearance from the government."

"Sexy," she said as she settled on his lap.

"You're the sexy one." John buried his face in her long blonde hair and inhaled the spicy citrus scent. Then, he drew back the strands and nuzzled her neck.

Mariah leaned into his caress and tightened her

grip on his shoulders. Relaxed in his warmth, she gazed with half-closed eyes out the rectangular window over his desk at the plethora of visible stars. A sudden motion caught her attention, and she jerked forward, eager for a closer look. Nothing. She glanced up at the security cameras. The ones pointed in the direction of the barn pictured a figure dressed in a dark hoodie lurking close to the door of the breeding barn.

Startled by the image, she leapt from John's lap and shouted out a staccato warning, "Man. Man in dark hoodie. Possible prowler by the barn."

John whipped his wheelchair around and peered at the cameras for a few seconds, then stabbed the intercom button for Gavin's home office. "Gavin, cameras caught a suspected intruder near the breeding barn."

Mariah didn't wait for the outcome of the call and banged out the office door, gaining speed down the hallway until she slammed through the front entrance, almost breaking the glass.

****

"John, you two stay put and watch the cameras," Gavin replied and with a bark added, "and call the sheriff."

"Gav, Mariah went after him," John said in a hurried clipped tone. "Unarmed."

"For Christ's sake. What was she thinking?"

"Not thinking, bro. Pure instinct."

Gavin grunted and disconnected the call.

John's nervousness transmitted to Cosmo, who paced and scratched frantically at the door. "Easy, boy," John said, switching on his security cameras to night vision mode. *She is closing in on the tango, but there is so little ambient light. Does she realize she is almost on top of him?*

Gavin appeared in the camera view with his rifle in a high port position bearing a night vision scope. He crept with the stealth of a tiger in their direction, then hesitated, cocked his head, and listened. With the weapon shifted to a ready position, he crouched forward.

John peered into the screen, fixated on the escalating scenario. Did Gavin see Mariah in a bent run, sliding behind the thicket? She and the perp are almost parallel in those hedges. Would he mistake her for the perp? *I can't take the chance.*

With a firm tap on the automatic release button, the door swung open. And John issued the command, "SEEK." Cosmo bolted out like a rocket as he ran toward his target.

John held his breath until the blur of motion caught Gavin's attention, diverting his course to follow the dog. Cosmo, in hot pursuit, closed in on the guy in a matter of seconds and in one smooth leap, seized the man's arm in his powerful jaws. Stunned, the interloper spun around and fell backward with a thud to the ground. Cosmo snarled and continued to shake the man's arm even after he grabbed a chunk of wood and began hitting Cosmo on the head and shoulders.

"Nobody fucks with my dog." Enraged, John snatched up his handgun, slinging four letter words as he wheeled out of the house toward the commotion.

As John closed the distance to the barn, he witnessed Mariah body-slam the guy and knock the wood out of his hand. He rolled up seconds after Gavin arrived and commanded Cosmo, "RELEASE." Gavin then zip-tied the asshole's hands, yanked the guy onto his feet, and said, "I'll take out the trash."

Cosmo whimpered as he crawled to his owner. Alarmed, John indicated with his hand for the dog to stay. "Oh, buddy. Are you hurt?" Hearing his master's voice, Cosmo struggled to stand but faltered.

Mariah hurried over and asked, "Is he okay?" She squatted in front of Cosmo.

John shook his head. "I don't think so."

"The dirt-bag struck him with a heavy stick." She probed along the dog's skull and shoulders. "Cosmo has a bump on the back of his head."

Ariel lumbered up to the group circled around Cosmo. "What happened?" She scanned the group while spreading her legs in a wide stance, with her right hand supporting her lower back.

"Cosmo was struck in the head with a heavy piece of wood," John said in a low voice, his fists clenched tightly.

"Let's carry him into the barn to my clinic and I'll check him out." In her usual professional demeanor, she instructed Mariah to lift his head and shoulders while she hoisted his back legs.

John glanced between Gavin, with a vice-grip on the dumbass, and the two women already crab-walking to the barn. "I need to check on Cosmo."

"Go. I'll wait here with the douche bag for the sheriff," Gavin said.

With a sheepish tone, John said, "Yikes. My bad, calling now."

****

The next morning when John woke, Mariah was missing from his bed. He called her name but there was no response. He checked the pillow next to his. No note. Today was the day she returned to Texas. *I wonder if she decided this was all a mistake and slipped out early.*

Darkness etched his mood as he snatched the t-shirt hanging on the back of his wheelchair and tugged it over his head. He scooted onto the chair and spun toward the door when a cooing voice accompanied by the soft yipping of a canine reverberated from the front room. *Cosmo and Mariah bonding.* A smile spread across his face. His mood lifted.

With his arms extended he called out, "Cosmo" and like a flying trapeze artist, a blur of sable-colored fur landed in his arms, licking his face, his tail wagging back and forth so hard his hind legs danced the tango. "Good boy."

"Your sister says he got knocked loopy, but he'll be okay," Mariah said.

"Is that a vet term?" John said with a snicker.

"Very funny. And Gavin got a report back from the sheriff. The dude we caught last night is part of the group stealing horses and skinning them. He cut a deal and spilled his guts. These guys are going down."

John continued rubbing his dog's ears. "That's great news. The entire equine community has been in terror since this ordeal started. I'll send over my surveillance tape to the sheriff's office." He steeled himself. "You scared the crap out of me, by the way."

"When I chased that bozo?" With a sassy flip of her wrist, she planted her left hand on her hip. "'Cause, you know what I do for a living."

"Well, yes, that, but I was talking about this morning when I woke up and you weren't here."

"Oh. Did you think I would leave without saying goodbye?" A frown deepened her brow as she splayed her hands.

John sensed her disbelief and impatience. He backpedaled. "There was no note."

"I wanted to surprise you. And just so we're clear, I'm as steady as the Northern Star, big guy." She held his gaze until her eyes misted over. "We both knew when I got here that I'd have to leave. We both understood I'd have to return to Texas."

"I'm sorry I doubted you."

"Don't make it any harder on me." She stared at the floor, and her shoulders drooped. "My body has to board that plane but my heart's not going anywhere."

"What time is your plane out of Orlando?" He forced his voice to stay even and without emotion despite the urge to scream, "Don't leave."

"It departs at three, so I have to be on the road soon. I'm already packed, and the rental is loaded. I've thanked Ariel and Gavin for their hospitality," —she chuckled— "and an exciting visit. The only thing left is our goodbye."

"I'll see you off." Stoic was his go-to, and he wore it like a Kung Fu Master. He told himself this was only temporary. With his security job for Wellington Farms completed, his schedule was free, at least for now, to visit Mariah in Texas. He had the will, so there'd be a way. In the meantime, there was Skype.

Mariah sauntered to the car and leaned her back against the driver's door. Her hands were trembling as she leaned down to pet Cosmo. "Goodbye, best boy. I'll miss you."

John handed her a khaki-colored case. "This is for

you." He squirmed in his seat as she opened it.

"What's it for?"

"It's a compass. The one I used in Afghanistan. I never got lost."

"I see that, but why a compass?"

"So you can find your way back to me."

Mariah clutched it to her heart. "I love you, John Armstrong." She kissed him long and hard, then climbed into her car.

As she drove down the driveway, Cosmo whimpered until she was out of sight.

"I know, buddy, I know."

Chapter Nine

Mariah grabbed her cell phone from her back jean pocket. She'd promised John she'd let him know she arrived home safely. For someone who'd been in a man's world competing as an equal she didn't need anyone protecting her or fretting over her safety, but the gesture was sweet. John was different, in a good way, from other men she'd dated. Rather than be threatened by her strong will and need for independence, he embraced those qualities. Maybe because his older sister possessed them in spades. Then there was Gavin. Once she penetrated his no-nonsense exterior, she discovered a down-to-earth man whose light-hearted banter challenged even the brightest mind. They had rolled out the red carpet for her and made her feel like one of the family. She couldn't wait to go back. After a quick text to John that she was safely on her doorstep finished with triple hearts, she entered her apartment and gasped.

Tizzy was working at her computer wearing a violet-colored cashmere sweater that resembled the one her mother had given her for Christmas last year.

"Welcome home," Tizzy said with a smile. "Good trip?"

"Is that my sweater?" Mariah dropped her bags on the floor and shut the door.

"Oh, this?" She slipped her palms down the front

of the fabric. "Er, uh, I didn't think you'd mind."

Heat surged through Mariah's neck. *Never mind that my mother probably paid two hundred fifty big ones for that sweater.* "I'd appreciate it if you'd ask first next time."

Tizzy splayed her hands with apparent nonchalance. "No problem."

Mariah eyed the large mug of hot chocolate next to Tizzy's mouse pad and visualized the chocolate cascading down the front of the fragile material. "Would you mind taking it off now?"

Tizzy's mouth slackened in disbelief and Mariah could have sworn a spark of anger flared in her roommate's eyes before she lifted her arms and tugged off the pullover. She tossed the crumpled top to Mariah. The swing went wide, and her elbow knocked the mug off the table. Chocolate fluid flowed from the mug onto the ivory carpet.

"See what you made me do?" Tizzy said, fuming.

"What *I* made you do?" She shook her head. "Really, Tizzy?"

Silent, Tizzy slid from the chair, avoiding the pooled chocolate, and headed for the kitchen.

"I'm going to drop my bag in my bedroom and then I'll come help you." *Mainly because it'll be my deposit that takes the hit for damage.*

****

Tizzy searched the contents under the kitchen sink for carpet cleaner and rags. "Hmmm. My bossy roommate must spend all her money on nice sweaters. Nothing here to clean a carpet. Soap and water will have to do." She grabbed a small bucket, filled it with cold water and squirted in dish soap before stepping back into the living room. Mariah was already on her hands and knees spraying the spot from a blue can. A pile of white rags lay next to her. *Always so perfect. I wish I could be more like her.* She set the bucket down and picked up a rag. "This was all I could find."

"Oh, thanks. We can use it after I get the surface spot up." Mariah kept scrubbing.

Tizzy grabbed a rag and started to scrub. "Why don't you go unpack. I can handle this."

Mariah glanced at Tizzy as she climbed to her feet. "I'm not upset, Tizzy. It was an accident." She grabbed her suitcase and lugged it into her bedroom, closing the door behind her.

Tizzy shrugged her shoulders and sneered. "Accidents just have a way of happening around me."

****

Mariah yawned as she entered the headquarters parking lot. Up past her normal bedtime, she'd skyped on her phone app with John the night before, for several hours, as if they hadn't just spent the weekend together. She never mentioned Tizzy on her Ocala visit but decided to use John as a sounding board. When she relayed some of her roommate's antics, the first thing out of his mouth was, "When is your lease up?"

She answered, "Two months and counting." Hesitant to elaborate that she didn't quite have enough for a down payment on a house yet, she'd left it at that.

Frank must have seen her arrive as he bolted out the back door of the building before her car jerked to a full stop, waving as he approached.

She parked and rolled down the driver's side window. "Hey, boss man. Are you happy I'm back?"

"Of course." He opened the door. "How was the

77

conference?"

She stepped out, retrieved her backpack from the backseat, and slung it over her shoulder. "Very informative and fun. I met some dudes from Orange County who included me in all the activities. They really made me feel welcomed."

"I heard." He grinned, extending his hand to indicate she should step ahead of him.

"What?" Mariah asked, a slight frown creasing her forehead.

"My counterpart from the Orlando district called me and forwarded the rave reviews from their senior attendee, a guy named Chad."

Heat raced up Mariah's neck and face. She quickened her pace toward the trailer and, glancing back, said, "Chad was very friendly," —she cleared her throat— "and, and, certain of himself."

Frank's shoulders shook with laughter as he caught up with her. "I see."

Mariah punched his arm. "Nothing happened." *At least not with Chad.*

"I believe you. Your business is your business. And speaking of business, let's step inside your office." He opened the door and held it for her.

"She stepped inside. "Thanks." After slinging her backpack onto the bench next to her desk, she plopped in her swivel-backed chair. "So, what gives?"

In his usual straightforward style, Frank said, "We were able to trace the partial tag you got from the black SUV."

"And?" Mariah said, her eyes wide.

"Stolen."

"What about the car at the park?"

"Nothing. Total blank."

"Where does this leave us?"

"Watching your back. That's where."

"I appreciate that, Frank, but you can't be my nursemaid twenty-four-seven."

"Nope, but when you're on duty, you're riding with a partner."

"Who is the victim?" She tried to lighten the tone of the conversation.

"Not funny, young lady." He swept off his cap, ran his fingers through his hair, and replaced the hat before continuing, "Tommy volunteered."

"Tommy. The mother hen, huh? Did you have to twist his arm?"

"No, ma'am. He's a team player and at the top of 'my guys I trust' list. You know, Mariah, the world is changing and not for the good. What happened to you is a sample of the way it's drifting. Law enforcement has become a slippery slope. I've been thinking about making it mandatory to ride with a partner. No exceptions."

"You don't think this is a freak thing directed solely at me?"

"Not entirely. Tommy's wife received condolence roses while you were in Orlando with a note that implied the two of you are having an affair."

"For Pete's sake, then why partner us up?" She bowed her head for a few seconds, then gasped. "Oh, crap. I need to call Susie before she comes after me with a kitchen knife."

Frank thrust his hands in a stop gesture. "No, you don't. Tommy assured me he and his wife are solid."

Mariah buried her face in her hands and mumbled,

"This is me hiding my embarrassment." She glanced up. "I hope you and Susie know I would never date a married man or my partner or my married partner. Geez Louise."

"Totally. I know you're squared away in that area and Tommy assured me Suzie knows this was a cruel hoax." He patted her on the shoulder.

"We're also beefing up security here at headquarters and I've asked the sheriff to assign a deputy to cruise your apartment every night."

She started to object. "The sheriff doesn't need—"

He shushed her. "It's already arranged. Does your apartment building have cameras?"

"No, but it's a gated complex."

Ignoring her comment, he said, "Consider getting cameras installed."

Mariah nibbled at her nails, a nervous habit she claimed helped her think but one she'd been unable to curtail. She dropped her hand. "Will do."

Frank squeezed her shoulder. "We will find out who is behind this and prosecute them to the fullest extent of the law."

Mariah's phone rang. She glanced at the caller ID and murmured, "Mother."

"You should probably take the call," he said while nodding at the phone.

Mariah lifted an eyebrow and in a lowered voice said, "Clearly, you've met my mother."

She answered, bracing herself for the onslaught of questions about her trip. "Hi, Mama."

He mouthed the words, "Good luck," before scurrying out the door like a squirrel chasing a nut.

With a shaky voice, her mother said, "Mariah,

thank God you're back. I think somebody pushed me down the back porch stairs."

Chapter Ten

"Oh my God, Mom. Where are you?" Mariah's heart raced as the unexpected news sunk in and a flood of adrenaline surged through her body. Hands shaking, she scrambled for her car keys and purse.

"I'm at Franny's house. She found me."

The whimper in her mother's voice tripled her anxiety. "I'm on my way. Put Franny on the phone, please." Gravel sprayed from beneath the tires as she exited the headquarters parking lot.

"Mariah, she's bruised and sore but fortunately she caught the handrail on her way down, which softened her fall. I don't think anything's broken, but she mentioned bumping her head, so I recommended she get checked out at the emergency room. I was going to take her, but she insisted on waiting for you."

The relief that surged through Mariah was palpable. She blew out a big breath. "I'm on my way." She ignored the yellow light and sped through the intersection. "When did this happen?"

"Late this morning. I phoned her several times, but the answering machine kept clicking on, so I rushed over and knocked on the front door. When she didn't answer I went around back and found her face down. Thank goodness the weather hasn't turned cold yet."

"Thank goodness is right." She slid her hands up and down the steering wheel. "Franny, Mom mentioned the possibility someone pushed her down the steps. Did you see anyone else around the house?"

"No, but she said the same thing to me. That's why I took her to my house."

"I see." She checked her watch. *Someone could still be in the house.* I'm going to check out her place before I come over. Do me a favor?"

"Sure, anything"

"Go ahead and take my mom to the regional hospital emergency room. Tell her I'll meet you there. And, Franny, tell her it's not a request."

"We're talking about Kathleen, your Irish mother, correct?"

Mariah chuckled. "Bribe her if you have to."

"Otherwise called a mocha latte." Franny snickered. "See you in a few."

****

The sun's final rays dipped below the horizon as Mariah rolled up to the curb two houses down from her mother's address, shut off the engine, and paused. She peered through the twilight, as she visually scanned the street in both directions, before focusing on her mother's residence. Nothing seemed out of place. Several random cars parked across the street had no visible occupants. After snugging her bulletproof vest and checking her weapons, she exited her SUV. She wanted to appear causal in case any of the neighbors were peering out their windows.

Neighbors. I need to interview the neighbors.

The front door was locked. *Dammit, I left my key in the truck.* She leaned back and checked the front windows. No signs of forced entry. With methodical thoroughness, she circumnavigated the house, checked each window, and finally arrived at the back porch. Her mother didn't usually lock the screen door but did keep an extra key under the bright orange flowerpot, in case she got locked out. Lifting the bottom, she ran her fingers along the edge. No key. She picked up the pot and groped underneath but still no key.

Hmmm. Maybe Mom hid it somewhere else.

Not wanting to waste time searching for the missing key, she jogged back to her truck, retrieved her copy, and returned to the back door. With a quick glance around, satisfied no one was watching, she withdrew her weapon from the holster and entered the dark house. With her 9mm in her right hand, she flipped the kitchen light switch with her left index finger. She cautiously swept the area with the muzzle of the gun before stepping into the open living area and repeating the same action. After clearing each room in the exact manner, she concluded there was no current threat and holstered the weapon. Nothing appeared out of place, damaged, or missing. Something didn't add up. Although her mother did exhibit early signs of dementia, she wasn't paranoid. If she said someone pushed her, Mariah would uncover the truth.

She switched on the outside spotlights and relocked the house, before striding across the street to the neighbor with a bird's eye view of the house. No one answered the door. With her suspicion on a slow simmer, she returned to her car, made a U-turn, and headed to check on her mother. Note to self: where the heck is the spare key?

****

A hooded figure rose from the back seat of the inconspicuous sedan after the noise of Mariah's powerful SUV's V-8 engine faded. "That was close. The sassy bitch passed right by my vehicle when she approached the neighbor's house."

I didn't mean to hurt her mother. When that nosy neighbor banged on the front door, I had no choice but to escape out the back. If only the old bag had stayed asleep, I could have gotten what I needed from Mariah's room and left. No biggie. When I think about it, Mariah could have avoided this by not being so private. I mean, who isn't on social media spilling their guts about every aspect of their life? Too bad. I'll have to come up with a Plan B to get what I want. I'd better get outta here before I'm spotted.

****

The emergency room waiting area was full when Mariah arrived but that was Fort Worth on most nights. She scanned the room for Franny or her mother, but the seats were filled with a woman comforting her crying baby, two bruised and dirty cowboys catching a snooze with Stetsons lowered over their faces, and several men with no apparent malady.

The young Hispanic lady at the reception window offered her a warm smile and waved her over. "May I help you?"

Mariah returned the smile as she approached the counter. "Hi. I'm looking for my mother who arrived with another female about two hours ago." She glanced down the hallway for a possible sighting.

"What's her name?" The young woman typed in the recited information while peering at the screen. "Bingo." She flung her hand in the air as if magic had just occurred. "Kathleen Michaels." She scrutinized the screen. "She's in exam room number three waiting for the doctor to go over her CT Scan."

Mariah's stomach somersaulted. "I'd like to join her."

"Certainly. May I see some ID, please?"

As she dug around in her purse for her driver's license, the familiar ringtone of her cell phone interrupted her. She slid the phone halfway out of the inside pocket and briefly glanced at the caller ID. *John.* She held her finger over the accept button and hesitated. She combed her hand through her hair and glanced down the hallway. *I can't deal with anything else right now.* Then hit the reject button. "Thanks for checking." She slid the license under the plexiglass.

"Oh, no problem. It's hospital policy." She glanced at the screen. "You're listed as her emergency contact. I'll beep you in."

The sliding glass doors opened. Mariah stepped quickly to the designated exam room where the doctor was in progress explaining the test results. She plastered a reassuring smile on her face and entered.

Her mother blurted out, "Mariah, you're here," — and turning to the doctor, added— "that's my daughter. She's in law enforcement."

"Sorry for the interruption," Mariah said, offering a sheepish grin to the doctor, who appeared amused as he took in her uniform. With a small wave to Franny, she leaned down and hugged her mother. "Hi, Mom."

The doctor continued his explanation. "The good news is there's no concussion from your fall. You do have a Grade II sprain, which will need to be immobilized with a brace or splint for one to two weeks."

"Any possible side effects, doctor?"

"It can result in stiffness and reduced range of motion when you take it off. Plan on some rehabilitation."

Mariah started to speak but Franny squeezed her arm and responded first. "I can help Kathleen."

The doctor chuckled. "While you two work out who will help this lovely lady, I'm going to write a script for the rehab and go over any questions with her."

"Thanks, doctor." Mariah smiled and nodded, then addressed Franny. "Would you step into the hall with me for a minute?"

"What's up, dear?"

"I checked out the house and nothing appears out of place, but the spare key is missing. Do you have it?"

"No, but that, added to Kathleen's accident, seems strange." Franny rubbed her chin. "Maybe Kathleen hid it under a different pot?"

"I'll ask her, but something doesn't feel right." She chewed her nail for a second, then dropped her hand. "I'm going to have her move into my apartment. I can sleep on the sofa for a few days until I can figure out what in the world is happening."

Franny shook her head. "Let her stay with me. I have plenty of room and loads of time."

"I don't want to impose, Franny. She isn't always completely coherent and—"

Franny held up her hand. "She's my closet friend. Let me do this."

Mariah, unable to speak over the knot in her throat, grabbed the older woman and embraced her in a tight hug. "Thank you."

"By the way, you are definitely your mother's

daughter."

"Why do you say that?"

"Want to wager the first thing out of your mother's mouth when I tell her she's staying with me?"

Mariah snorted. "I don't want to impose?"

Kathleen exited the exam room in time to catch her daughter's comment. "I'm ready to go home, Mariah. Will you drive me?" She gingerly eased her sweater over her injured arm. "I don't want to impose any longer on Franny?"

"Like I said…." Franny snickered.

"What scheme are you two conspiring?" Kathleen swiveled her head between the two women.

Mariah ignored the question and instead asked, "Just curious, Mom, but did you take your spare key from under the garden pot?"

"Are you kidding me? I have a hard enough time remembering where I put things." She huffed. "It's under the same pot as always. Why?"

"No reason. I couldn't find it this afternoon, but I might have checked under the wrong pot."

"Well, silly. It's the orange Italian pot planted with the yellow geraniums."

Mariah and Franny glanced at each other with raised eyebrows before Mariah said, "Well, that's very specific, Mom."

Franny mouthed to Mariah, "My house," then put her arm around her friend and said, "I need a favor from my bestie."

Mariah teared up. Unable to speak, she patted her heart with her hand. With a smile and a wave, Franny steered her mother out of the hospital. Relieved her mother would be safely tucked away, she shifted her mindset to harness the simmering rage she'd worked hard to suppress. *I'm going to render this scumbag, whoever it is, impotent for messing with my mama.*

Chapter Eleven

"I've left two messages for Mariah and nada." John tapped his fingers in a rapid beat on the arm of his chair. "You think she changed her mind?"

"No way, bro." Ariel rested her elbows on the counter.

"God, I hate this."

"What 'this' are you talking about, little brother?"

"Not being able to reach her. Feeling like I'm trying too hard. I don't know."

"She's probably out of cell range, boarding boats, checking fishing licenses, capturing an injured owl…" Ariel added possibilities until John gave the time-out signal.

He snorted. "Whose side are you on?"

"Yours, baby brother. Always yours," Ariel insisted.

"See these gray hairs on my temple?" John touched his hair. "You should probably stop calling me your baby brother." Admittedly, he loved the endless banter with his sister, despite her apparent view of him as still a toddler.

"Not going to happen." She playfully thumped his head, then jerked her attention toward his computer screen. "Hey, a notification just popped up on your screen, boo-boo."

John whirled his chair around and viewed the

message. "It's Mariah. She wants to talk. Says it's urgent." His chest swelled. "She needs my help."

"Go. Be the hero you always are, John," Ariel said, wrapping her arms around his shoulders in a goodbye hug.

As soon as the door closed, his fingers flew. He texted, —I'm here.— Not waiting for a reply, he texted, —Phone or computer?—

—Computer. Want to see the full view of your face. Connecting to Skype now.—

John, stunned at Mariah's revelations about her mother, listened intently before grabbing a notebook and pen. "Mind if I take a few notes? I have an idea."

"No. What were you thinking?"

"Security cameras. I can install them at your mother's house. I also think we should put one in your bedroom and two in the front of your apartment building with a view of the parking lot and the stairs."

"Good idea. Would you recommend someone I can trust? I've run into some scammers out here while working my job."

"Yes. Me. I can come out this week."

A full minute of silence taunted John's worst fear. *She's embarrassed to introduce me to her friends, mother, co-workers, everyone.* "You still there?"

"John, I live on the second floor of an apartment building and there is no elevator."

"Whew. Is that all?"

"What?"

"I thought you were…never mind."

"Listen. I know it's screwed up, but the owners haven't upgraded the premises to comply with the Americans with Disabilities Act. They should have their asses fined."

"It's not a problem, Mariah. I have a work-around."

"What is it?"

"Not a what but a who."

"Stop the man speak and tell me the whole idea."

"I have a friend, former SEAL, K-9 handler, Mike O'Malley, who lives on the outskirts of Fort Worth in a small town named Weatherford. He trains service dogs and retrains former K-9s for civilian ownership. I can stay with him, and he can help me do the install."

Mariah stopped short of saying she didn't want to impose and instead said, "Cool. Bringing Cosmo?"

"Yes. I'll drive and provide all the equipment we'll need. I can be there in two days."

"Despite everything going on, I'm excited. You'll get a firsthand impression of my wacky roommate, meet my incoherent but lovely mother, and watch me get teased within an inch of my life by my male counterparts."

"Looking forward to it." He chuckled. "Not."

"You can always change your mind."

"Never gonna happen. Two days and a wake-up."

****

Mariah closed the top of her computer and checked her watch. *Getting late*. She ducked her head under the half-closed blinds in her office and peeked out the window. The glow of red, orange, and pink hues that highlighted the western sky gave her a sense of permanence. "The sun will rise, and the sun will set," she muttered.

Tommy stuck his head in. "Hey, troublemaker."

Mariah ignored his light-hearted tone and swiveled

her chair around so fast it almost tipped over. "Tommy, I'm so sorry for dragging you into this mess." She steadied the chair by grabbing the corner of her desk. "Do I need to call Susie?"

He laughed. "No. I filled her in."

"What did the note say?"

"Roses are for romance, these are a clue,

Your husband's cheating,

Feel sorry for you."

"I'm going to kill whoever is doing this."

"Oh, it gets better. They included a photo of us when our heads touched, trying to simultaneously put your suitcase in the trunk of my car."

Mariah screwed up her face. "I don't get it?" She recalled their heads bumping as they both dove for the luggage. "Whoever took that picture knows it was innocent but they're twisting it."

"Yep. Nasty stuff."

She started to apologize again but he stopped her, saying, "Let's get the motherfucker."

Chapter Twelve

"Why don't you have Gavin drive with you to Fort Worth and just fly back afterward?" Ariel asked.

Her tone conveyed worry. He didn't want her, or anyone for that matter, to worry about him. "He has a farm to manage. And you have Elmo—will have Elmo," —he extended his hands a foot from his belly— "soon."

Ariel rubbed her lower back. "You got that right. Ugh. He's gonna be a big 'un."

"So, it's settled. Cosmo and I leave tomorrow."

"Oh, I see what you did there. Nice try." She wagged her finger at him. "John, I swear, sometimes you forget you're," —she hesitated— "physically challenged."

John tightened his hands around the wheels of his chair. "I *never* forget, sis. I do, however, accept all challenges."

He perceived the mental struggle of his older sister because it was always the same. She wanted to protect him. She assigned herself responsibility for him. She didn't want to helicopter mom him. He was a grown man. The predictable conclusion took less than a minute.

"You're my baby brother, albeit a grown man, who is capable of making his own decisions."

He raised his hand. "No need to explain. I don't

94

want you to worry. Name your conditions."

"Not conditions, simply suggestions." She waved her arm with a flourish.

"Uh-huh. Whatever." He began stuffing items into his briefcase.

"Bessie Mae packed a cooler full of food and beverages for you to take. It'll limit the number of stops and expedite your trip."

He continued to pack. "Good idea."

"Keep your phone on and update us during your trip."

"Check."

"Don't drive straight through. Get a hotel halfway."

"Already have a reservation near Gulfport, Mississippi." He gave a thumbs up. "Confirmed access and service dogs okay."

"Carry your weapon. For emergencies."

"I never leave home without it." He held up a concealed carry case.

"Don't be a smart-ass."

"Now you've exceeded your," —his fingers fashioned air quotes— "suggestions quota."

****

Cosmo sensed a trip. John understood the unspoken signs of his companion's excitement. With his ears pointed forward, the dog sat like a statue in the front passenger seat while Gavin tucked him into his seat harness. John patted his shoulder. "Good boy." The German Shepherd responded with a quiver.

Ariel rested her arms on the open window ledge and said, "You're all loaded up. The cooler is in the back, fully filled." Then added as she took a step back,

"Safe trip."

Gavin double-tapped the side of the passenger door and slid beside Ariel, wrapping his arm around her shoulder. She leaned into his chest and smiled.

With a final glance in the back of his modified van to confirm all the surveillance equipment and needed supplies were on board, he nodded goodbye to the two people he loved the most in this world.

****

After two long days of hammering down the highway, John and Cosmo cruised into the city limits of Dallas just before nightfall. As the sun set behind the skyline, dotted with tall, modern buildings, multicolored lights flickered on across the cityscape, giving it a youthful vibrancy and pulsating energy. Traffic buzzed by as he slowed to view the plethora of looming green direction signs. He spotted the one for Fort Worth and exited off Interstate 45. Cosmo, always alert to any change, whined as he leaned into the turn.

"I know, buddy. You need to stretch your legs. O'Malley's place has lots of room. Not long now." He checked his watch. *Right on time.*

A few months ago, when he first talked to Mike about visiting, his friend told him the guest house had been upgraded with handicapped access. He explained many of the clients he dealt with were disabled veterans and needed service dogs to help them perform daily functions. Others suffered from PTS and the dogs served as emotional support. His joke was that dogs form a bond easily and are without the complexities of a human attachment.

"Said Mike, the man who's been divorced twice. Right, Cosmo?"

"Woof. Woof." Cosmo, paying full attention, tilted his head to the right.

John chuckled, then ran his hand over his bristled chin. He hadn't bothered to shave on the trip. In fact, he hadn't bothered to put on deodorant or do more than run his fingers through his hair because his canine companion could care less.

His phone rang and the name K-9 Mike lit up the screen. "Hey, buddy. We're about twenty minutes out."

"Cool, man. Thought you might be lost. No city lights out here."

"Nah. I'm squared away. This GPS is like a guided missile."

"Looking forward to getting caught up."

"Me too, man." He ended the call.

A short while later, the sign for Warrior K-9's Inc. lit by two spotlights came into view. John's headlights switched to bright as he turned down the dark, dirt road. He and Mike O'Malley went way back. They served together in Afghanistan. Combat develops a special comradery and the anticipation of connecting again made him giddy, like the first day at summer camp. The long beam of the headlights captured the outline of a lone figure at the end of the driveway waving him through the metal gate. As John passed through the opening, he realized the man he'd served with hadn't changed much, at least not physically. Now sporting a full black beard and a tad bigger around the waist, he still exuded Alpha confidence. Mike hand signaled John to park in front of a nearby ranch-style house, then jogged behind the van until John braked.

As John unsnapped Cosmo's seat belt, the driver's door flung open. Mike, never one for small talk, grabbed him into a bear hug, then slapped him on the back.

"Good to see your ugly mug, man," John said, a warm smile spread over his face.

Mike lightly shook John's shoulders. "Hey, pretty boy. Who you calling ugly?" He fashioned a mock pose with his hand on his hip and his eyes raised, fluttering his lashes.

While John grabbed his sides laughing, Mike surveyed the inside of the van. "WOW. Quite a rig. The VA spring for this?"

"Thanks for my service." John snorted. "Adaptive hand controls, rails on the doors for easy entry and exit and check this out." John reached into the back and retrieved a seat cushion, two tires, and a lightweight wheelchair. "A travel chair with quick release tires so I can load it myself."

"Slick, man." Mike smoothed his hand over the frame. "And there's Cosmo, being cool as a cucumber. I'll bet he's hungry. Grilled burgers for dinner. Made an extra one for you, buddy. Get 'um while they're hot."

Cosmo, trained to wait for the command 'friend,' didn't wait. Instead, he leapt over John, hitting Mike square in the chest before he bounced onto the ground, spinning in excited circles around the man who saved him. Mike knelt and hugged the dog's thick, wooly neck. "Hey, buddy. It's been a while since I found you skulking at my gate."

"His lucky day," John said as he rolled around the bumper of the van, "and mine."

"Hungry, hair wet, all matted." Mike shook his head as he stood. "God. Who in his right mind abandons a dog this smart and handsome?" He stroked the length of the German shepherd's body.

"No one sane." Cosmo took a position next to John and sat. "Check it out." John chuckled. "He's patiently soaking in the two humans extolling his virtues."

"True. This guy reads people like a body language expert." Mike continued eye contact while he fumbled around in the back of the van and dragged out John's duffle bag. "I take it his training went well?" He swung the bag over his shoulder and motioned them forward.

"The guy you referred possessed some serious canine mojo." John rolled in beside his friend, keeping pace as they headed toward the house.

"Yeah, ex-military dog handler, same creds as me."

"But *not* you, Mikey. Still, the fact he could work with us at the farm was convenient."

"Win-win." Mike squeezed John's shoulder. "Let's eat, then you two get a good night's sleep before we tackle why you're here."

Chapter Thirteen

John woke early and sent a quick text to his sister, assuring her he arrived without mishap. Last night would have been better but he and Mikey drank beer and swapped war stories around a roaring fire pit until after midnight. Cosmo, tuned-in to John's apprehension around fire, paced between the flame and the men but eventually assumed the chill demeanor of his charge, and snoozed at their feet.

—*Glad you arrived okay…you little moppet.*—

He returned her text with three heart emojis, then leaned back and chuckled at what he pictured would be her exasperated head toss.

His phone dinged. —*Your emoji game is strong, bro.*— He was certain there was an added head toss.

The anticipation of his next call dropped a thirty-pound dumbbell to the pit of his stomach. He was in her world now. Would he meet her mother, partner, boss, roommate? Did they even know about him? Did it matter? To him it did. His fear of maneuvering over a canyon catwalk was miniscule compared to the trepidation twisting his insides of how this visit might unfold.

Get your head straight, man.

He checked his watch. *Getting late. She's expecting my call*. He tamped down his anxiety and punched in her number. It rang once.

"John, you're here." Her voice rose with excitement. "I can't wait for you to meet everybody."

His doubts evaporated. "Yeah, that'd be nice." *Focus on the mission. Protecting Mariah.*

"How was your trip?"

"Uneventful."

"Do you want to meet for an early lunch?"

"Sure."

"How's bar-b-que sound? I know a great little dive close by my office."

"Love the Q."

"I'll text you the address."

"Mind if Mike O' tags along?"

"No, I'd love to meet him, but why?"

"I want him along for reconnaissance of your apartment as well as your mother's house, which I'd like to do right after lunch."

"That'll work. My boss approved my leave request for the afternoon."

"Too bad we can't spend the afternoon alone, together. I'm waggling my eyebrows. Fill in the blank."

She started to speak but belly-laughed instead. "Oh god, only you can make me laugh about something as dark as being stalked." Her voice softened. "Thanks."

"You're welcome. By the way, how is your mother?"

"Oh, she's getting bribed with lattes at her friend, Franny's house." She exhaled an audible breath. "She's safe."

"Good. I'll grab O'Malley and head your way."

"See you soon."

"Mariah, we're going to catch this psycho."

"I believe you."

****

Mike slid his chair back from the wood table and patted his stomach. "That was the best bar-b-que I've had anywhere around Fort Worth. Thanks for the tip, Mariah."

"Yeah, well, leave it to the guys I work with to locate all the 'best eats' joints." He picked up a small chunk of meat and held it above Cosmo's head. The dog immediately sat up on his hind legs. "I see you haven't forgotten any of the tricks I taught you."

"He's out of practice but his memory rivals an elephant's," John said, his comfort level off the charts. Mariah and Mike really hit it off.

"We better get going," Mariah said. "I'll text Tizzy in case she's at the apartment and let her know we're on our way."

"I suggest you not," Mike said as he slowly shook his head.

"Why?" Mariah crossed her arms over her chest.

"Need to know and she doesn't need to know," John chimed in.

"I realize she's a little kooky but it's her space too. Doesn't she have a right to know we're putting cameras in and around the apartment?"

"Number one—your safety is my primary concern. Number two—I've never met her, so I don't know what her level of kookiness is. Number three—for emphasis, your safety is my primary concern."

"Okay, okay. I'm tracking." Her gaze dropped to the floor and she shifted uncomfortably, as if embarrassed. "I did notify the management company for the complex and they approved the cameras."

"Big whoop. They'll be installed so no one knows

they're there, right, Mikey?"

"The point, bro."

****

When they arrived at the apartment, Mariah's stomach gurgled and rolled as she scanned the parking lot for Tizzy's car. She had mixed feelings about installing the cameras without telling her roommate, but she trusted John's experience. Surveillance and intel had been his specialty in the military. His unit tracked down more than one Taliban terrorist. This stalker had nothing on him. Her stomach settled. "Tizzy's car is not here but I don't keep track of her schedule. She could come back at any moment."

"Okay. Let's not slow roll this." John opened the side door of the van, lowered the ramp, and rolled onto the pavement. "O'Malley, you're up. Do the inside cameras first. Mariah, go with him. Cosmo and I will hold point while we set up the computer relay here in the van."

"What kind of car does she drive?" John asked.

"A black MINI® Cooper hybrid."

"Easy to spot. Got it." John seated his headset, then buried his face into his computer.

Mike adjusted his companion headset, then picked up a large black duffle bag and nodded to Mariah. "Right behind you."

She jogged ahead across the parking lot and straight up the stairs, key in hand. After they were inside, she pointed to her room and stepped aside. "What can I do to help?"

Mike's head swiveled around her bedroom until his view landed on a colorful painting hanging in a large wooden frame on the opposite wall. "There."

"My woodland watercolor?"

"Yep. My small camera is the same color as the frame. I can tuck it in the corner."

Mariah's mouth gaped open as she peered at the tiny size of the camera he removed from his bag. "I'm going to remember that thing is there when I undress."

"Ah, c'mon, give the boy a break." Mike laughed as he climbed up on a chair, then stepped atop the dresser. With drill in hand, he had the install done in less than fifteen minutes. "Testing," he said aloud into the microphone of his headset. "Can you see everything in the room?"

Mariah couldn't hear John's response but from the broad smile on Mike's face, she guessed there was a comment attached to the fact he nailed the camera placement. A mental twig snapped as she stared at the camera. Her desire for independence and need for privacy evaporated.

"May I?" She pointed to the earpiece.

Mike stepped off the dresser to the chair and handed her the device, a big question mark on his face. She situated the earbud into her ear and said in her best Texas drawl, "Repeat after me, cowboy. The images captured by this camera will be viewed by you and only you and will never end up in a text, on the internet, or in any man cave, *ever.*"

"Babe. I would never."

"Even if we had a bad break-up?"

"What? Not happening," John said. "At least not from my end," he added, a noticeable edge tinted his tone.

Mariah caught Mike out of the corner of her eye, tiptoeing out of the room, and pinned him with her tone,

"Where are you going?"

"Oh, snap." He stopped and turned. "I wanted to give you two some privacy." He rubbed his hands up and down his face. "Mariah, I'm going to say this once and I'll give it to you straight. I served with John. I've seen him operate in the worst kind of conditions, against unimaginable evil and he didn't break. Didn't quit. He won't violate your trust, even if you toss him to the curb and break his heart, which I hope you don't…" His eyes turned dark, and his jaw twitched in a steady beat as he continued, "because I'd personally post those images on the cover of the New York fucking Times."

The verbal reprimand from the normally mild-mannered dog handler stunned her into silence and woke her to the reality she'd let the stress get to her and mess with her judgement. *John had no nefarious intent.* Ashamed of her reaction to their obvious attempts to help her, she muttered, "Nerves." Then, for John's ears, she repeated, "Nerves, I'm a bundle of nerves. I deserved that."

"The words were muffled but the tone wasn't. It appears you got one of The Big Guy's patented ass-whoopings," John said.

"You got that right." Mariah tittered. "Here's Mike."

Mike slipped the headset on and said, "We good here?" He listened, smiled, and nodded, then glanced sideways at Mariah.

With two thumbs up, she said, "All good. Let's get those other cameras installed pronto before we tackle the outside cameras."

"Your girl's good. Coming out," Mike said as he

swung the duffle bag over his shoulder.

Despite or maybe because of the earlier beat-down, she and Mike worked well as a team and had the project completed in less than an hour. No doubt she was in good hands with these two.

As they started toward the van, Mike halted abruptly, and leaned into his headset, then swung his arm in front of her. "Say again?"

"What's up?" she muttered.

He whispered back, "Trouble." After disconnecting the call, he explained John observed a blonde driving a black MINI® Cooper at the security gate. "We need to get back to the van and haul ass out of here before she sees us."

"Tizzy is a definite brunette." Confused, Mariah added, "but we need a plan before she sees us. She has a suspicious nature and John was adamant about keeping her in the dark."

"Paranoid, probably, but either way, we're out of here. Why don't you distract her while I zip to the van?"

"I'll need a cover story as to why I'm here without my car." She noticed his puzzlement. "Small parking lot. She'll notice the absence of my car."

"Meet your friendly pick-up driver who will provide transportation back to the service station where your car is getting a flat fixed." Mike tipped his imaginary hat.

"Good thinking. Go down the back stairs and I'll head her off out front."

Mariah hopped down the front stairs and waited for Tizzy to come into view. Was she wearing a blonde wig for some reason? Trying not to overreact, she adopted a poker face as Tizzy bounced toward her, blonde tresses falling around her shoulders. The motion didn't flow like a wig. Why would she change her beautiful auburn hair color?

"You been to the hairdresser?" Mariah asked, hoping to prompt an answer.

"You like?" Tizzy flipped her hair over her shoulder.

"It's the same blonde shade as mine…I guess so. But why? Your hair color was so rich and showed your Irish."

"Well, don't blondes have more fun?"

Tizzy's flippant response and the fact she ignored the why question annoyed Mariah. *First my sweater, now this. What next?* "Not always."

"Hey, what are you doing for dinner? We could go out and test the theory." Tizzy giggled.

Mike approached with perfect timing and yelled, "Fred's pick-up service. Your car is ready."

"I can take you and then we can go out," Tizzy said, moving between Mariah and "Fred."

"Oh, I can't tonight. I need to check in on my mother."

"Is everything okay?"

Acting on a gut reaction, Mariah decided Tizzy didn't need to know details about her mother's accident. "She had a little spill but she's fine. I just want to check in."

"You're a good daughter." Tizzy smiled.

Fred cleared his throat. "Got a schedule to keep, Miss."

"Later, Tizzy." Mariah waved as she followed "Fred" to the van. Fortunately, John had turned it around so all Tizzy could see was the side door. She hopped in the front while Mike entered through the back door.

"Roommate's a babe but kinda' sketchy," Mike said flatly.

"How so?" John asked.

"Tizzy dyed her hair blonde like mine because she thinks blondes have more fun."

"Well, as the famous quote goes, 'imitation is the sincerest form of flattery,'" Mike said with a sardonic roll of his eyes.

Mariah noticed John staring at her. "Like I said, Tizzy is quirky and sometimes annoying but she's harmless."

He arched an eyebrow and put his hand on her legging bobbing like a boiling egg. "Really?"

She put her hand on top of his and squeezed. "Yes, now let's hustle our butts over to my mother's house."

Chapter Fourteen

John brushed his palms together. "That's the last install." He rolled back to survey the group's handiwork on Mariah's mother's house. "Great team effort, guys."

"Excellent work, lads," Mariah said. "I owe you two a dinner."

Mike and John exchanged glances. "I have dogs to feed," Mike said. "Rain check?"

"Sure." Mariah nodded. "We'll drop you off at the ranch."

"Thanks, but I'll Uber back." Mike, phone in hand, dialed. "You kids have fun."

Mariah swept her hands through John's hair. "Mind if we stop by my office?"

"No, but I was hoping for a little us time."

"My plan also. We have all night." She leaned in and whispered in John's ear.

"Is that your wish list?" John tilted his head toward her and waggled his eyebrows.

"Yes, in any order."

"I'll drive."

"I'll try and keep my hands to myself."

****

"Liar," John said as he drove into the unpaved parking area behind the Tarrant County Law Enforcement Center.

Mariah straightened her blouse. "Who me?" She flipped the visor down and checked herself in the vanity mirror.

John followed the point of Mariah's index finger and stopped in front of a new double-wide trailer. "Yes, you who shoved my hand up your blouse."

"I kept my hands to myself. I didn't say anything about *your* hands."

"Semantics." John laughed, then shifted his gaze forward to the building in front of him.

"Hey, lights are on in the office."

Mariah checked her watch, then glanced around the lot. "Boss is here." She tilted her head toward an official suburban in the otherwise empty lot. The words embossed on the door in a circular design read, Game Warden. "Working late, I guess."

"Cosmo and I will wait for you in the van." John stretched back and rubbed Cosmo's head.

"Chicken," she teased as she opened the side doors and jumped out.

"Oh, hell no." John shifted into his wheelchair and slapped the large chrome button marked 'ramp'. As the metal unfolded, so did John's nerves. To say Mariah admired her boss was an understatement. More like worshipped. She valued his opinion and, despite her deeply independent streak, she listened to his advice. What if he didn't think an injured combat vet was the right guy for his protégé? Would he tell her to ditch the disabled dude?

Mariah gave a nod of acknowledgement to the man standing statue-like on the deck, at the top of the trailer entrance, then addressed John. "You'll like him. I promise." She started up the pathway, then paused.

"Go ahead. I'll catch up." He noticed her hesitation. "Shoo." He waved his hand, motioning her forward. "You too, Cosmo." The dog circled John twice, then trotted after Mariah.

By the time John approached the pair, they were engrossed in a choppy back and forth. Not wanting to eavesdrop, he stopped at the bottom of the incline and whistled for Cosmo.

They both spun around in the direction of the shrill call, allowing John to view Mariah's flushed face, all screwed up in a frown. Her sunshine had converted to no bueno in less than sixty seconds. *What's wrong?* Frank's weathered face bore dark circles under his eyes. *Uh oh. Is he putting the big kibosh on our relationship?* John gripped both wheel rims. *I'm not going down without a fight.* He didn't wait for an invitation and wheeled up the slanted ramp. With all eyes on him, he suffered a smile and stuck out his hand. "Hi, you must be Frank. I'm John Armstrong." He studied the man's demeanor with an unflinching gaze.

Mariah rocked back on her heels and stuffed her hands in her pockets. "Finally, you two get to meet." She squeezed John's shoulder in a reassuring gesture and smiled.

Frank gripped John's hand and pumped his arm in a firm, friendly handshake. "Nice to meet you." His tight smile along with the somber mood eased. "Mariah's been singing your praises."

A sly grin crept over John's face. "You can sing?"

"Smartass," she said as she lightly smacked his shoulder, then twisted toward Frank. "See what I put up with?"

Frank smirked but ignored her question. "And by

the way, thank you for your service, John."

"My pleasure." He liked that he had managed to lighten the mood, but he wanted in on whatever was going on. He also liked the direct approach. "So, what had you both grimacing like you stepped in a pile of dog poop?"

Mariah worried her bottom lip as she squinted at Frank. "Go ahead. Tell him."

"Out of concern for recent events, I assigned Mariah a male partner. Tommy's a good guy, reliable. Been with the department a long time." Frank bowed his head and intertwined his hands across the back of his neck. "Ugh." He dropped his hands and eyeballed John. "The son of a bitch came after him."

John leaned forward and met Frank's stare. "What happened?"

"Tommy's brakes mysteriously went out on his drive home. He crashed into a hedge. On purpose. Better than a brick wall or cement divider but still, banged him up pretty good."

John caught a glimpse of Mariah as she swiped at the corner of her eye and lightly touched her hand. "How do you know it wasn't just a mechanical failure?"

Frank withdrew a note secured in a zip lock bag from his pants pocket and held it out for John to read. "This note left at the scene after the accident and while Tommy was unconscious rules out any coincidence."

As John scanned the note, his grip on the wheels of his chair tightened, bulging his forearm muscles. *Mariah belongs to me. Back off. This is your only warning.* With his heart pounding against his ribs, he gathered every reserve of calm. The message smacked of evil and left no doubt all the previous incidents were personal. This was more than simple payback from a drug runner arrested by fluke when Mariah asked for a fishing license. This was a directed attack. Well-planned with the flair of "obsession"? He wondered if the person was anonymous or someone familiar to Mariah. An old boyfriend?

"Honey, can you think of any exes you dumped who didn't take it well?" John said, his voice steady to hide his all-out panic that some crazy psycho wanted to take her away from him.

"Heck no. What kind of asshole would do something like this?" Mariah said. Her strained voice rose to a high pitch as she continued. "I can't even think of any of the perps I've arrested who would stoop this low. Most of them are hunters without licenses or fishermen who caught more fish than the law allowed. Even when alcohol is involved, they usually apologize for their laxness and pay the fine." She splayed her agitated hands, before thrusting them through her hair.

It pained John to witness his lover's distress over her partner's accident but experience told him to drive forward. With personal discomfort equaling a sand spur between his toes, he doggedly pursued his line of questioning. "What about enemies from the job? Gotten anyone fired lately?"

She screwed up her face. "No way."

"I've contacted Deputy Sheriff Graves," Frank said, taking control of the conversation. With an aside to John, added, "He's the deputy assigned by our local sheriff to investigate Mariah's first incident."

"You think they're all connected?"

"Yes, I do."

"Even the break-in at her mother's house?" John's instincts told him absolutely, but he wanted to test Frank's savvy.

"My gut and the timing both tell me one nasty sociopath is lurking behind a mask of deception somewhere."

This guy's good. But before he could agree, Mariah strode down the ramp.

"I'm going to the hospital to check on Tommy, y'all." She stopped at the bottom. "Then, I'm going home to warn my roommate." After a glance around the parking lot, she heaved a deep sigh. "John, will you drive me?"

"Of course. I'll be right there."

In a deep voice, he informed Frank he'd be driving Mariah straight to his friend Mike's ranch for the time being and that he'd be staying for a while longer. "I'll text you the address."

As Frank gave a thumbs-up, John's phone buzzed with the receipt of several downloaded texts. He ignored them and turned to join Mariah. The familiar tune of The Good, The Bad and the Ugly blared from his phone. He told himself to stay focused. Without checking who the caller was, he dropped the cell phone into his over-the-shoulder concealed carry bag. He'd listen to his voicemail later, after he had Mariah safely tucked away. Nothing short of a death in the family would interrupt his mission to protect her.

****

"Hey, you missed the turn for the hospital," Mariah said, twisting her neck as they flew by the illuminated exit sign.

"We're not going anywhere near the hospital,

sweetheart. I'm taking you to Mike's for the night."

"The hell you are." She fisted her hands. "Pull over, right now."

"You need protection," he said, his eyes straight ahead. "I learned the hard way to ignore situational awareness."

"Oh, and you've decided with your pumped-up ego you're the man to do it?" She seethed.

"Yes," he said in a firm but soft voice. "This is my area of expertise." He glanced over and noticed her rigid pose, her squared shoulders, and ramrod straight backbone. Certain adrenaline surged through her stress-induced body dictating combat mode, his best option was not to engage. Her words stung but they wouldn't deter him from doing everything in his power to ensure her safety.

"Did it occur to you I can take care of myself?" She pursed her lips into a tight line.

Determined not to take the bait, he responded with an affirmative nod and hit the gas.

"That's it? A freaking nod?" She grabbed the steering wheel, veering the van into the next lane. "Let me out." A hard thud sounded in the back seat as Cosmo slammed into the floorboard.

"Stop, Mariah!" he said as he steadied the swerve. "Cosmo, forward." The dog dutifully stepped between the two humans, providing a barrier.

John surveyed the landscape ahead and noticed signs designating a park. Checking the rear-view, he crossed the two lanes to the exit and smoothly rolled down to the well-lighted parking area. After shifting into Park, he cut the engine and reached for Cosmo. In a practiced procedure, he ran his hands along the dog's side and down each leg.

"You good, buddy?"

Cosmo rested his head on John's leg while his tail thumped against the seat. "Okay, then, good boy." He rubbed Cosmo's ears. "You're tough."

Mariah tilted forward to pet Cosmo, but John blocked her hand. "Don't." *She's been begging for a fight. Now she's going to get one.* "He wasn't in his safety harness because I was so out of my mind worried about your safety, I forgot." She started to speak but he placed his index finger to her lips. "I'd be dead if it wasn't for this dog. His unwavering loyalty and trust are beyond the capability of most humans. He's been my whole life," —he choked on a sob, gulped, and continued— "until I met you."

****

Mariah lifted his finger away from her mouth. "I'm sorry, so sorry. I know what he means to you. I'd never want to see him, or you hurt." She clutched her heart and started to weep.

"I'm already hurt, Mariah, permanently broken. Is that why you didn't think I could protect you?"

"God, no. Is that what you think?" She choked back more sobs.

"It occurred to me, yes."

"Well, you're wrong. Truthfully, I have never experienced the kind of care, concern, and interest in me, rather than sex, from a man, like I have from you."

"Not even your father?"

"My father was indifferent toward me. He wanted a boy—a namesake, someone he could go hunting and fishing with. Someone to whom he could pass on his cruel, inhumane methods."

She crossed her arms as her lips twisted into a deep frown. "He forced his warped ideology on me. That legacy haunts me to this day."

Mariah realized her breathing had become strained. She panted for air. "It's why I became a game warden. To protect animals against unlawful and unethical practices."

"And you're a total badass at your job. Me wanting to protect you doesn't diminish that."

"Growing up with my father was like growing up without a father, so I learned to be independent."

"I get it, totally. I grew up without a father. He served as a Marine in Beirut and was killed there while my mother was pregnant with me. Ariel took over after our mother died and helped raise me."

"That explains your closeness. You're lucky. I'm an only child."

"Let me protect you, please."

"I will but I want a compromise. Trust me to go back to my apartment. I promise to be extra careful, but I'm concerned about my roommate. She's a nice girl but very ditzy and lax on security. She could be in harm's way, like my partner, and she doesn't deserve to get caught in the middle of this."

"Counteroffer. Go warn her to be extra safe and then stay with me tonight at Mike's. It'll give me a chance to test the cameras."

"Deal." Mariah glanced at John's phone, vibrating in his lap. "Someone is blowing up your phone."

John leaned in for a kiss. "First things first. We good?"

Mariah's lips met his. "Mmm. Swimmingly." On cue, Cosmo whined and lightly pawed her leg. "Oh, you want a kiss too?" She laid a light peck on his extended nose.

John's shocked expression as he checked his text log alarmed Mariah. "What is it?"

"Bessie Mae died. A sudden heart attack." He grimaced. "My sister asked me to drive home for the funeral." He gazed up at Mariah. "I'll tell them I can't leave."

"No, you must go back. This is a tragedy for your family, especially Gavin. The magnitude of how much he lost must be crushing him. Ariel filled me in on the role Bessie Mae played after his mother died. She was center pole in that circus tent." She gazed at him with raised eyebrows. "And based on the wild and wooly tales your sister relayed of Gavin's misspent youth, Bessie Mae was juggling a three-ring circus."

"My place is here with you. Gavin's no longer a troubled juvenile delinquent but a former SEAL. He can handle this."

"Probably but I don't want Gavin or Ariel resenting me because you wouldn't be there for them. I'm asking you to go home. I have protection from the sheriff and my fellow officers. You can keep an eye on me from Ocala via the cameras."

John banged his fists on the steering wheel. "What a shit show."

"I'll be fine." She squeezed his leg. "I don't want you to worry."

"Why don't you come back with me?"

"You know I can't do that."

"Frank would approve a leave under the circumstances. Guaranteed."

"He would but I'd be leaving my team in a lurch.

We're already shorthanded with wardens being shuffled to the border."

John cupped Mariah's face. "You're a good person."

"So are you, which is why you're going to be with your family and offer your support while I perform my official duties here in the great state of Texas."

"Now you sound like a politician." He tugged her ponytail and huffed.

She checked her watch and gasped at the late hour. "How long have we been parked? I guess I lost track of time and forgot about dinner. My car is still at the restaurant, and it closes soon." Mariah inhaled a deep breath after realizing her sentences ran together like one giant freak-out.

"I'll take you to your car, then go back to Mike's and pack," John said as he turned the ignition and backed out of the parking space without so much as a smile in her direction.

"Are you okay?"

"Not really, although I realize you're right." He sped onto the freeway. "This is the rational, logical solution, but I don't like it."

"You don't have to like my suggestion but I'm asking you to do it."

"I'll go for you, but you can't make me like it."

"I love you."

John stewed for a minute and then said, "I ride at dawn."

Chapter Fifteen

The hooded person read the incoming text and typed a reply. —Good job on completing your task and delivering the note. Now, maybe they'll listen to me.—

The reply read, —Awaiting my reward. Where and when? I'm horny.—

A sly smile spread across the figure's lips. *I've got you right where I want you. You'll be begging for it.* With fingers flying, the reply was typed and sent. —Same place, tonight at eight. Bring wine.—

After selecting their conversation, the disguised creature chose "delete" and "all" before tapping the delete button a second time. As the conversation disappeared, a slight snicker erupted in a satanic fit of glee. *Just like he's going to do after I get what I want. Then one day when Mariah and I are finally together, I'll tell her how much I sacrificed for her. The clown helping me carry out my plan doesn't want money. I'm the preferred method of payment. When I'm getting humped tonight, I'll close my eyes and pretend it's Mariah.*

****

After retrieving her car from the restaurant, Mariah stopped by the office, then returned to her apartment, anxious to alert Tizzy to the potential risk of being her roommate. When she entered the living room, curtains were drawn, and the lights were off. Even the night lights, perpetually on, had abandoned the space. The smell of licorice permeated the air. An eerie feeling clawed at her gut. *Am I in the wrong apartment?* She flipped on the cheap overhead chandelier and scanned the room. Everything appeared the same except an added emptiness dominated the space. John's visit seemed like merely a minute while he was here but since he left, now approached an eternity.

Tizzy's door was closed. *Was she here, asleep?* Mariah checked her watch. *After ten. Late, but she's usually awake at this hour working on her computer. Hmmm. Who knows. I haven't been around much lately. Maybe she finished the project she was working on.* The smell of Anise drew her into the kitchen where a mostly empty uncorked bottle of Ouzo and a half-filled glass of the same lay parked on the counter. Waving her hand over her nose, she corked the bottle and emptied the glass. She glanced back at Tizzy's door and decided to wait until morning to have their talk. A good night's sleep worked wonders when the topic bordered on this level of bizarre. She'd give Tizzy the option of finding another, maybe safer, place to live which would mean she'd have to bite the bullet and pay all the expenses for the next two months until her lease expired. Or Tizzy could opt to stay at her own risk. The choice was hers.

As she entered her room, she waved and gave a thumbs-up sign, yawned, and stretched wide before plopping down on her bed. *This could be fun.* Certain John was already asleep and had not had time to review the cameras, she decided to give him a show. Something to keep his mind on her. She studied her iPod and set the music to the soundtrack from *Fifty Shades of Grey*. As the music started, she freed her hair from the ever-present scrunchie, which kept her long locks out of the way in a back-and-forth toss. With a wink in the direction of the camera, she kicked off her boots and peeled off her socks. Next, she licked her lips and slowly unzipped her pants, shifting from right to left leg as she lifted the pants in the air, twirling them with a final sling to the opposite corner of the room. She kneeled on the bed facing the frame with the hidden lens and clasped her bosom, so her cleavage protruded from the top of her blouse. With both hands, she drew the blouse over her head, gyrating her hips as she progressed. Attired in her underwear and bra, she wiggled to the end of the bed and slithered up and down on the bedpost, tilting her head back, allowing her hair to fall the length of her back.

Although a rank novice as a pole dancer and first-time exhibitionist, she hoped John appreciated her effort because it stirred desires she'd never experienced before. She released a seductive moan. So engrossed in her own sensuality, she didn't notice Tizzy standing in the doorway until the song changed.

A slow, heavy hand clap jerked Mariah's attention. "OMG." In a gawky retreat, she unwrapped her leg and fell backward onto her butt with a thud. With several forward scoots, she grabbed her iPod and shut off the music.

After brushing the blonde strands off her flushed face, she struggled to explain. "I…I… shut my door." She snugged her shirt to her chest. "I didn't know you were home. Or maybe asleep." With her free hand splayed, she added, "Spur of the moment."

"I only caught the end." Tizzy flipped her hair over her shoulder. "The door *was* closed but music at this hour? So out of character for you, so I peeked."

"What if I hadn't been alone?"

"Well, you've never invited anyone home and, in fact, you were alone." She tilted up her chin. "Weren't you?"

Mariah cringed at the thought of Tizzy's potential reaction if she revealed the presence of a camera, much less all the camera locations. What would John's reaction be when he found out she broke her promise to him? Either way, she'd need her muck boots to wade through the level of shit she'd be in. While her thoughts warred, she scurried around the room, scooping up her clothes and boots, buying time. Tizzy wasn't having it.

"Is there someone special you're showing off for?"

Mariah, noting the edge in Tizzy's voice, opted for the direct approach. "Yes. A guy I met on ForeverThe One.com dating site. You know, the one you encouraged me not to join." She chuckled to lighten the mood. "Thanks, by the way. Oh, and he installed a camera here in my room."

"Wait a minute. You hooked up with a guy? When?"

"Recently." Hoping to keep it vague she added, "We've skyped and when he learned of my apparent stalker, he arranged for a camera to be installed in my room."

"He was here? In the apartment?" Shock paled her face.

"Not exactly but close enough." *With every question and answer, I'm perilously close to betraying my agreement with John, but Tizzy has a right to know she's now in the threat circle.*

"I'm sorry I haven't set you straight on what's been

happening. My excuse is I believed it was work-related and only recently realized what's going on overflowed into my personal life and could potentially put you at risk."

Mariah patted the side of the bed indicating Tizzy should sit. "You have a right to be read in on what's going on so here goes." Tizzy parked herself on the edge of the mattress and crossed her legs.

Mariah proceeded to explain the reasons behind all the mystery surrounding her recent business trip but withheld the details of where she went or the succeeding trip to Ocala. When she relayed her suspicions about her mother's accident, Tizzy's calm acceptance of the potential danger mystified her. Not the reaction she expected. Nor was Tizzy's outright refusal to end her sublease early. She claimed she was sticking 'til the end. Had she misjudged her roommate? Airhead was Mariah's original impression of the woman but maybe she was simply an introvert and not empty head space.

With the idea of ending on a positive note, she divulged her relationship with John, relishing in relaying his experience as a combat veteran, a war hero who owned a successful security business. She didn't mention his disability as it no longer mattered. She regretted he had to return home early, denying them the chance to meet. Oddly, Tizzy didn't pepper Mariah with questions about her new love. Instead, she grew strangely quiet. Mariah found herself lost in the moment as she extolled John's virtues until she noticed Tizzy's clenched fists. Guilt rode her like a wild monkey. She'd never intentionally hurt someone without justification, but the defensive pose of her roomie indicated she'd done exactly that. Cognizant Tizzy used work as a substitute for a social life she'd babbled on and on about her newfound love like there was no tomorrow. The conversation started out friendly enough, but when the topic turned to John, Tizzy shut down. She blamed herself.

She folded her hand over Tizzy's fist. "Enough of me droning on and on about John." She stood, drawing Tizzy to her feet. "Hey, I need to check in with the office, but I'll be home later."

"I liked hearing about him. He sounds perfect." Tizzy flicked a particle off her blouse, then straightened the material over her jeans. "I'm sure there'll be a next time to meet him." She smiled before moving to the door where she paused. "Later."

"There's ice cream in the freezer." Mariah offered with a smile as she partially closed the door.

"What kind?" Tizzy called through the crack.

"The yummy kind," Mariah said light-hearted, happy the conversation ended on a high note.

With a quick glance at her phone and half smile toward the camera, she tossed on her clothes. A phone call with John was what she needed right now. She wanted a hug, but she'd settle for small talk and maybe a little reassurance after her show. With a shouted goodbye to Tizzy, who had disappeared into her room, she rushed out the door toward her car. A quiet drive on the back roads with John's voice purring in her ear, talking future and his next visit sounded better than a bubble bath and a beer.

Chapter Sixteen

John viewed the small crowd in a semicircle around the gravesite. As the casket lowered into the grave, Gavin dropped his head onto his chest. Tuned into his most subtle indicators, Ariel tucked her arm through his and stepped closer. She'd always worn the protector hat. Protector of all things she loved in this world. He thanked his lucky stars for her.

Gavin's shoulders shook as he swept away tears. Knowing Gavin, they were unwanted and uncomfortable tears. He'd exhausted his capacity for grief over teammates killed during the war or from their suicides after returning home. His frequent talks with Gavin around the kitchen table accompanied by Bessie Mae and a plate of her homemade cookies, helped ease the pain. Few knew she'd served in Vietnam as a combat nurse. She shared their reality. Bessie Mae would be missed.

After the minister bestowed his final blessing, the crowd dissipated. Gavin shook hands with him, then nodded to John, indicating he wanted to get out of dodge. *I don't blame you, brother.*

The car drive back to Wildwood was uncomfortably quiet. Gavin, who usually blasted country music, set the tone with radio silence. Stone-faced, his jaw set, he clasped the steering wheel in a death grip. Ariel stared out the front window of his truck. One hand rested on her belly while her other hand, using the window ledge, propped up her head. Even Cosmo declined to hang his head out of the open window and inhale the multitude of enticing country smells. Instead, he rested his head on John's lap, eyes flicking back and forth between the three passengers. Mindful of Gavin's propensity to bottle up his feelings and tough it out, no one ventured into conversation. No reason to let that genie out of the bottle.

When they arrived home, Ariel asked him to join them in the main house for lunch, but he begged off the invitation. With Bessie Mae gone, the kitchen would be a hollowed-out space. Besides, he didn't want a sandwich. What he wanted was food for the soul. Time for a chat with Mariah. He hoped she liked the 'missing you already' card he dropped in the mail on his way out of town. Corny? Maybe, but it served as a physical link between them across time and distance. Although he didn't mind being alone, loneliness was an entirely different emotion. The events of today had rammed home that difference. He fired up his computer and security monitors for a quick quality control check. He'd have heard from Mariah if there'd been a problem, but a routine review of the footage was part of how he handled his job.

As the recording rolled, his mouth gaped open. He tilted his head as if viewing the image sideways would make more sense. His heart raced. Sweat popped out on his forehead and "WTF" escaped his lips. Mariah had undiscovered talents. That was for sure. He kicked himself for leaving and missing out on a live, in-person show. He'd beg for a redo. He fished around for his phone with his eyes glued to the monitor.

"Uh-oh," he said as Tizzy popped into view. With no sound, but judging body language, he could only guess what the spacey little twit was saying to Mariah. When the conversation finished and Tizzy exited the room, his arousal devolved into embarrassment. He averted his gaze as Mariah dressed and switched views to the living room. Mariah passed through to the front door in a rush and left the apartment. On a gut feeling, he continued to watch. Tizzy peeked out from her partially opened door and scanned the living room. Then, she crept along the walls with a sharpened focus on the framed art. With meticulous pursuit, Tizzy checked every corner and peered behind each frame.

"What is she doing?" He continued to observe as Tizzy peeked under the shades of the floor and desk lamps. "Are the bulbs burned out or," —he cringed at the thought— "is it possible she found out about the cameras?" It was after she dragged a step ladder over to the chandelier and climbed to the top rung that he realized she had somehow found out about the cameras. Her frustrated eye roll and squinty-eyed scan of the room from her perch told him she missed Mike's careful placements.

"Jesus. How did she find out? *I don't believe Mariah would break her promise to me.* Why would she tell her about the cameras?" Heat surged up his neck. "She can't be that naïve. Can she?"

He steadied his hand and reined in his temper before he punched 'dial' on his phone. *I want to hear her reason for breaking her promise to me.*

She answered on the first ring. "John, good timing. I was calling you."

"Is there something you want to tell me?" he said

Forever the One.com

with purposeful control.

****

Her job in law enforcement had exposed her to every kind of weirdo. There wasn't much that got her panties in a twist. Drunk deniers, (no, ma'am, I haven't been drinking), expired fishing licenses, (oh, do I need a license to catch bass?) and her favorite; naked, horny teenagers aroused in the back seat of a car, (We didn't hear you, didn't see you there.)

"Yes, there is." She gushed. "I miss you so much. You're the most normal person I know."

"I miss you too but that's not what I'm talking about."

His formal tone lacked the usual ease and signaled something was wrong. Uncomfortable with his stiffness, she exhaled a deep sigh and asked the obvious question, "What's wrong?"

"Tizzy is what's wrong. I checked the cameras this morning and caught her snooping around the apartment. She rivaled the FBI in her search of the living room before climbing on a stepladder and examining the chandelier."

Mariah gasped. "Oh no. The cameras."

"Good thing she's short 'cause even on tiptoe she couldn't see over the top of the fixture."

"You don't think she found any of them?"

"Judging from her behavior I'd say her sleuthing came up with a zero."

"Thank goodness. What happened?"

"Nothing, really. Rather blasé attitude afterward. She returned the ladder to the kitchen pantry, grabbed her phone and purse, then left the apartment."

"Well, no harm done, right?" *He knows. God, I feel*

129

guilty. I need to 'fess up. She wiped her moist palms on the steering wheel. "I know why you called," she said, her voice barely above a whisper.

"Did you tell her about the cameras?"

Mariah's eyelids fluttered as she sat up and gripped the steering wheel. The question landed without inflection, a statement rather than a question. *Busted.*

She couldn't lie and ruin a perfectly awesome relationship. "I did tell her about the camera in my room but only after she ambushed me during my, er, uh, performance, meant exclusively for your eyes."

He made a growling sound. "You broke your agreement with me."

"I didn't mean to."

"Are you insane?" he thundered. "Or just incredibly naïve?"

"Wait just a minute, John. I made a judgment call. You're overreacting."

"You have someone out there who is so obsessed with you that he almost killed your partner and likely had something to do with your mother's accident. I'm not overreacting."

She'd always valued her independence, her ability to take care of herself. She vowed never to need a man but only to want a man. Her visceral reaction to John from their first encounter tattooed her heart with a magnetic pull. Was she about to blow it with the first man she'd desired in a long time? Maybe ever? He was clearly pissed, a side to his personality she'd never experienced, but was he overreacting or was she underreacting?

"I told her about the one camera in my room."

"Like that gets you off the hook for breaking your

agreement with me. This is about trust, not cameras."

"You can trust me."

"Can I?"

She could feel him slipping away. "I'm sorry. I panicked when I heard her clapping."

"Here's the thing, Mariah. I learned the true meaning of trust in combat when you trusted the guy to your right and the guy to your left with your life and they reciprocated." His voice thickened with emotion as he continued. "We can't have a relationship without implicit trust."

"John, I get it. I do. What can I do to make this right?" Panic twisted her gut. She'd gone from heaven to hell in thirty seconds flat. "You can trust me. I promise."

He cleared his throat and hesitated before he answered. "You broke your agreement with me. I don't take that lightly and neither should you, but I understand you've been under enormous stress lately. I believe you. We'll chalk this up to extreme extenuating circumstances."

"You got that right." Mariah's voice cracked. "With everything that's been going on lately, my castle walls are crumbling." Her chest heaved up and down in labored breathing.

"I'm here, Mariah," —His voice deepened— "and my shoulders are broad."

"I know you are and, and they are." She glanced at the dial with a shallow smile as tears welled in her eyes, blurring her vision. It was only a matter of seconds before the tears would turn into a shameful torrent. With a hard grip on the steering wheel, she searched both sides of the highway for a place to pull off. A vacant strip mall appeared on the right and promised privacy. She sped up on the approach to the exit and with the tires squealing, made the turn into the parking lot. As she eased into a parking space at the end she blurted out, "Handling crazies."

She choked back sobs, then continued. "I can do my job but when my family is the target of crazies…."

"Did something happen to your mother?"

Mariah ran her hands under her eyes and inhaled a deep breath. "Thank goodness, no. In fact, she's begging me to let her return to her house. She misses her garden and I think the familiarity. The fact someone might have 'helped' her or tried to hurt her to get at me is unnerving. I feel helpless." Her breathing shortened into jagged gasps. "I'm a wreck."

"Deep even breaths." John's voice soothed her. "I'll check the cameras for her house. If there's been no activity and the increased police patrols are still active, I don't see a reason she can't go back."

"Okay."

"Feeling better?"

"Yes." She leaned her head against the headrest and closed her eyes. "You have such a calming effect on me."

"Baby, your safety is my number one priority. When I instruct you on a security procedure, you can bet it's for your protection against a cunning, ruthless, highly intelligent enemy. I'm not trying to control you or dominate you or be your boss."

Her heart might burst. She couldn't remember a time she loved anybody more than she loved this self-possessed man. He was right about trust being the foundation for any good relationship. He didn't play games. Neither would she.

"I admit I've taken the threat too lightly. I was wrong to think I could handle this on my own. I need you. When are you coming back? I need a hug. Like a bone-cracking bear hug."

"Hugs I can do," John said. "Would you settle for a swaddling hug? I don't want to hurt you."

Her voice husky and suggestive, she offered a few 'hug' positions and ended with, "All night long."

He wolf-whistled. "Packing as soon as we hang up."

Chapter Seventeen

One Month Later

John stared at the trail of heart and kiss-face emojis spilling across his phone screen. He honestly didn't think he could get luckier or more aroused. The girl of his dreams was sexting him daily with promises, promises, and oh my lord, promises. There'd been a time in the not-too-distant past when doubts about ever finding true love clouded his mind and kidnapped his hope. With all his failed efforts on the dating site, he'd convinced himself happiness only favored the whole, the complete, not the broken. His projection of himself as damaged goods accompanied him on every date and set him up for a self-fulling prophecy of being without a mate for the remainder of his life.

Mariah changed the loner scenario in a righteous way. Before he knew what hit him, she'd flipped his mindset upside down. She never allowed him the luxury of self-pity. She wasn't careful with him, but she always had his back and he loved her for it.

When he had to delay his trip back to Texas to attend the trial of the scumbag who killed several valuable horses, she didn't give him a hard time. She supported his decision and helped the prosecution with a videoed testimony about her apprehension. Despite the large pile of turd events on her plate, she never tried to guilt him about the delay. Lord knows guilt was his middle name. Determined to make up for missed time, he selected a heart emoji followed by, "Take a gander out your front window," and hit send.

****

"You finally made it," Mariah said, throwing her arms up in a hoorah. She stepped from the porch of her office and descended the ramp.

"Better late than never," John bantered as he propelled his wheels forward.

"Yes, *but* the early bird gets the worm. Ha. Two can play that game."

"Are you calling yourself a worm?" John sputtered.

"Shut up and kiss me." She kneeled on one knee, then briefly examined his face. "You're so pretty." With her hands steadied on his cheeks, she pursed her lips against his.

He moaned and cupped the back of her neck, tightening his grip as his tongue slipped past her lips, igniting a rhythmic tongue tango.

Lost in the heat throbbing between her legs, the approaching thumps on the wooden slats of the ramp didn't register. But the gruff, noisy sound of someone clearing their throat landed like a hammer in her warm, carnal space, "Harrumph."

Startled, Mariah sprung apart from their embrace and lunged for the handrail, missed, and toppled backward onto her butt. "Frank, I, I didn't know you were here today." A hot flush shot up her neck and covered her face.

John, a broad smile on his face, held out his hand, "Frank, nice to see you again, um, anytime."

Frank threw his head back in a loud laugh, then

135

shook his head. "I guess love knows no bounds." He glanced around at the surrounding government offices and employee parking lot. "Literally."

Mariah stood and dusted herself off. "Geez." She pointed at herself. "Color me embarrassed."

John grabbed her hand. "Color me happy."

"Glad to hear it. Hey, where's your dog?" Frank glanced around the immediate area.

"Oh, Cosmo wasn't feeling well so I left him with Mike. It's a rare occasion to be apart but I didn't want to delay seeing Mariah."

"Oh no, what's wrong with him?" Mariah wrung her hands.

"A little car sick after the long trip. He'll be fine."

"That dog has quite a few frequent flier miles at this point. I'm sure he'll be okay." Frank put his hand on Mariah's shoulder. "Did you tell him the good news?"

"He is the good news, boss." A broad, ear-to-ear smile stretched across her face, crinkling her eyes with joy.

"I mean the other good news." Frank chuckled.

"I'm all ears," John said. "Let's hear it."

"The police caught the guy who sabotaged my partner's car. He's a known gang member whose fingerprints were on file."

Frank added, "He got sloppy and left a print at the accident."

"That's awesome news. Has it been determined if the break-in at Mariah's mother's house and the other incidents are connected?"

"He confessed to the car chase and shoot-out at the pier as well as the park hoax but says he knows nothing about the mother or the photo and letter to the partner's wife."

"Hmmm." John scratched his chin. "I'd feel better if we could connect those things."

"He admitted to trading sex for his dirty work but claims he doesn't know the mystery woman. Apparently, she contacted him for hire. One gander at her had him hot to trot. He wanted sex in lieu of money."

"What the fuck? That good, huh? Did he give you a description?"

"Yes, but she sounds like a generic twenty-something brunette with a pixie cut. We have a police artist working with him, but he's a career criminal and reluctant to help law enforcement unless he gets a sweet deal."

"Well, get the DA to give him a saccharin sweet deal. I want this piece-of-shit caught."

Mariah exchanged glances with Frank, then explained, "The DA is reluctant to offer him anything due to his yard long arrest record for drug smuggling and human trafficking."

"Typical bull hockey."

Mariah laid a hand on his shoulder. "Easy, cowboy. Let law enforcement do their job. We'll catch her."

"Something about this scene smells like week-old fish."

"What do you mean?"

"How did he contact her? Where did they have their trysts?" John's voice grew more intense with each question. "What was her motivation for all this?"

Frank stepped in, "All good questions which we will get the answers to. For now, the best thing for you to do is keep monitoring those cameras and alert us if you see anything suspicious."

John nodded, then turned to Mariah, "In the meantime, I want you relocated to Mike's ranch where I can keep an eye on you."

"We'll talk," Mariah said.

Chapter Eighteen

The hooded person, savoring the smoky taste of a cold beer, glanced toward the dim glow of the television atop the bar. With the volume turned down, it was hard to make out what the talking heads were saying until an image flashed on the screen. A loud crack as the glass mug slammed against the wood counter, followed by, "Oh crap," caught the attention of the bartender. He hurried over, cotton rag in hand and patted the spilled beer pooling along the edge. The figure swatted at his hand, pointed toward the television, and jerked her thumb up repeatedly, signaling him to adjust the sound.

As the bartender increased the volume on the remote, the reporter's voice rose to an audible level. In a monotone voice, the young newscaster spouted confirmation of the arrest of a known gang member who allegedly traded sex for crimes against local law enforcement officers. *I can't believe the dumbass got caught. UGH. I gave him strict instructions. Typical guy thinking with the wrong head. One thing's for sure. I need to cover my tracks and get rid of all potential connections to my identity.*

The figure slid off the bar stool, drew the hood of the fitted jacket lower, then slapped a twenty-dollar bill on the counter and strolled out of the one-star tavern. With a quick glance in each direction, and a flick of the wrist, the burner phone was dumped in a curbside trash can, leaving four missed calls ignored.

****

John gazed at Mariah while she slept next to him. It had been a long month without smelling the floral scent of her hair. As he slid his finger along her soft thigh, his crotch tightened but he welcomed the familiar ache that always accompanied any physical contact with his sex queen.

He wanted to wake up every day next to her but hadn't convinced her to join him permanently at Mike's yet. For now, their rendezvous at the upscale Hilton in downtown Fort Worth proved the perfect romantic venue.

There'd been no work incidents for a month, so she didn't see the necessity to "hide at Mike's fortress." Her words. Besides, she'd argued, he'd eventually have to return to Ocala and the ranch was a long way from headquarters. Then, he'd point out her lease was up for renewal soon and rents had skyrocketed. Tizzy's decision to relocate closer to her office would leave Mariah without a roommate. He drove his argument until he got 'the look'. Time for a more subtle strategy.

A beautiful, three-year-old female German Shepherd named Artemis had arrived at Mike's ranch for rehabilitation into civilian life. She'd washed out of the Homeland Security program for bomb-sniffing dogs. Too skittish in busy airports and big city noise but ideal for country life, companionship, and protection. Mike suggested Mariah would be the perfect fit. He agreed and swore Mike to secrecy.

The new plan involved Mariah eventually joining him in Ocala. He believed deep down she was ready to make the change but her strong need for independence as well as undying loyalty to her game warden pack kept her from committing. She had all the best reasons for not relocating, a mother who was mentally failing and a promising career she loved. He hoped asking her to marry him and the promise of a life together would be enough to change her mind.

"What are you thinking about?" Mariah propped up on her elbows.

Mesmerizing sapphire eyes greeted his gaze. "You're awake."

"Awake and satisfied." She leaned against his arm and cooed.

"You wanna super-size that satisfaction?"

She slapped his arm. "Very funny."

"Ouch." He scrunched up his face. "Careful. I'm delicate."

"No, you're not." She laughed and squeezed his eighteen-inch bicep.

He lifted her hand from his muscle and kissed her palm. "We still on for dinner with the roommate tonight?"

"Yes, and Tizzy was insistent on treating."

"Uh oh, what does she want?" He smirked and arched an eyebrow.

"To win you over? To celebrate the purchase of her first house? I don't know. Can't it simply be a kind gesture?"

"I have my doubts."

"You have such a suspicious nature, John. Don't try to get out of this. As I told you, there's been much less drama and things have been going better. We've even had a few dinners and Dutch trips to the bar."

Despite his successful avoidance of spending time with Mariah's looney roommate, he'd agreed to her invitation to dinner tonight. It wasn't that he totally hated Tizzy but her deference toward him seemed like an act. What was more annoying was her constant fawning over Mariah, who handled it with aplomb. Still, Tizzy's clinginess bothered him.

****

The tension between John and Tizzy manifested itself by way of an invisible band tightening around her forehead as she cross-flowed their increasing antagonism toward each other. The pressure grew tighter and tighter until a wicked headache formed. She'd made numerous attempts to diffuse Tizzy's passive-aggressive digs and John's bluntness, but it was as if she wasn't even there. Cosmo's presence would have helped diffuse John, but Tizzy was on a roll and there was no stopping her.

Her intention for a friendly dinner slid into an unmitigated disaster as they competed about what she needed and wanted. No one asked her what she thought. "Hey, y'all are stressing me out. Knock it off."

"Help me out, Tizzy," John said, ignoring Mariah's origination. "I'm trying to convince Mariah to live on Mike's ranch."

"Hey, guys, stop," Mariah pleaded as she rubbed her temples.

"She doesn't need to leave our apartment." Tizzy showed Mariah the palm of her hand and continued in a snide tone, "The perpetrator was caught."

"Not so fast. There's a female accomplice still out there," John shot back.

"Hello? Neither of you are asking me what I want."

142

She stood and positioned herself between them, then added, "I'm capable of making my own decisions."

Tizzy stepped around Mariah. "I can take care of Mariah while we're roommates."

"Oh, another month? Then what?"

"Then you'll be back in Ocala." She smirked. "She can move with me into my new house."

Mariah's head pounded and her stomach heaved. A sour taste pervaded her mouth as bile crawled up her esophagus. Releasing the grip on the chair she leaned on for support, she scanned the restaurant for the restroom sign, then rushed toward the entrance, her hand clasped over her mouth.

****

John, alarmed by Mariah's color-drained face and abrupt exit, rolled away from the table in pursuit when his wheelchair was jerked to a stop. Tizzy stood behind him clutching the back frame.

"Hey, let go." He twisted in his chair to face Tizzy. "Something's wrong with Mariah." He grabbed the wheels and engaged in a tug of war, determined to break her grip.

Tizzy leaned in and whispered in John's ear, "News flash, bud. She confided in me about how she really feels about you."

"What are you talking about?"

"Mariah confessed she isn't interested in a long-term relationship with you."

"That's a lie," he replied flatly.

Tizzy ignored his assertion. "Because you're confined to a wheelchair, you'd prevent her from living the life she deserves."

John's gut twisted as if a knife had been shoved

into its core. He glanced toward the bathroom before he faced her. "That's bullshit."

"Oh, Mariah swore me to secrecy but it's all true." She jutted her chin as she crossed her arms across her chest.

Her smugness exhibited the satisfaction one might experience after shoving her worst enemy off a bridge, but he held his ground. "We'll see how true it is when Mariah returns."

He observed a telling twitch on the corner of Tizzy's mouth right before she loosened her grip on his chair.

"She'll deny she said it if you ask because she feels sorry for you, but she said it."

Out of the corner of his eye, he caught a glimpse of Mariah in the seconds before she stood in front of him, a greenish pallor etched on her face. "You okay?" he said, barely able to get the words out. He cleared the hoarseness from his dry throat. *Could my stress load be any higher?*

"Not really feeling so great. I'd like to get outta here."

"I think we're finished, right, Tizzy?" John glared at her. When she stepped back a pace, he was certain she got the double entendre he intended.

"Thanks for treating us, Tizzy. Sorry to ruin the meal."

Tizzy peered at John from under her eyelashes, then smiled at Mariah. "The pleasure was all mine."

****

Five minutes into the drive back to Mike's, Mariah couldn't stand the silence any longer. John's pale face and hollow stare out the front window alarmed her.

She'd never seen him exhibit such a deer-in-the-headlights expression. "What happened while I was in the bathroom?"

"What happened to our vow to be honest with each other?"

"Wow." She shook her head. "I'm not a shrink but Tizzy obviously upset you. Spit it out, mister. What did she say?"

"I'll tell you but swear you'll tell me the truth."

"Always."

"She said you divulged you aren't interested in a future with me." He clenched his upper lip in his teeth and smacked the steering wheel. "The fact I'm disabled will prevent you from living the life you deserve." He glanced at her. "Did you say those things?"

"I'm pissed." A hot flush surged up her neck and spread across her face.

"With Tizzy, I hope."

"With both of you. Tizzy because she acted so inexplicably savage and you…with the connection we have, how could you possibly fall for that lie?"

"I didn't. That's why I'm asking you."

"No, I had to pull it out of you, and just for the record, what she said doesn't contain a scintilla of truth."

"Good to know." He swallowed hard. "I love you and want you to have the life you deserve even if I'm not in it."

She placed her hand on his thigh. "I *am* living the life I deserve right here with you." She swiped at her eyes. A rosy hue returned to her lover's cheeks, and his eyes sparkled with life again. But Tizzy? What was that all about? She'd never seen a destructive side of her roommate. Tizzy was the intelligent introvert, a nerd who led a busy work life but a boring personal life. On occasion, she'd expressed envy of Mariah's full of action and excitement life. But why sabotage her relationship with John?

"What are you thinking about?" John caressed her hand.

"Tizzy." She shook her head. "I don't get it. You think she's jealous of you?"

"Of us. We need to have a serious talk about Tizzy."

"Oh, I plan to do more than that."

"No. Don't tell her I told you."

"What? Why not?"

"I've always gotten a weird vibe from her. Trust me. I'm missing something. But the cameras are still in place. Wait and watch."

"Agreed but with the addendum of coming to each other right away if someone tries to put a wedge between us again."

"One more thing. I want you to shelter at Mike's."

"I don't think it's necessary but if it'll make you worry less…."

"Well, I have a surprise for you waiting at the ranch that I think will tip the balance in my favor."

"What is it?"

"You got to see it."

"You know how much I hate mysteries."

He wagged his finger back and forth. "Not telling."

She laughed. "Were you on the debate team?"

****

Mike and Cosmo were waiting for them as they passed through the open metal gate. At first sight of the van, Cosmo spun in happy spins before dashing toward John's van. Mike saluted John and waved enthusiastically to Mariah. What a welcome committee. She really liked Mike O'Malley. He was a straight-up guy who obviously admired and even loved John. She understood why. And Cosmo? A lifesaving wonder dog who'd take a bullet for his owner. She didn't know much about German Shepherds before Cosmo, but she was sold on the breed.

"Well, he's happy to see someone," she said as she nodded toward Cosmo.

"You," John said.

She met his gaze as he focused on her mouth until interrupted by heavy panting. Cosmo hadn't waited for him to exit but bounded over and braced his front paws on John's open window ledge. With his tongue lolling out of the side of his mouth, he gave the impression he was smiling.

"You were saying?" She glanced at John. Crickets. Nada. He simply indicated for her to exit the vehicle.

After she rounded the rear of the van, Mike waved her forward, then turned in the direction of the barn. She quickly stepped in beside him and briefly turned back to locate John. "Where's my surprise?"

"I gave you a clue when I wagged my finger." He repeated the action.

Mariah gave him a withering stare. *I think he's enjoying pulling my chain a little too much.* She wrinkled up her nose and bit out, "I'll say it again. I hate mysteries."

When she turned back around, she almost tripped over the most beautiful German Shepherd she'd ever seen, sitting at attention, focused on her. "Oh my, Mike.

Is this your newest acquisition?"

"You could say that." He peered over her shoulder and winked at John.

Confused, Mariah checked John's reaction to the wink. He grinned and wagged his finger back and forth. She gasped. Was the magnificent creature intended for her? Hesitant to get her hopes up, she squeezed her eyes closed for thirty seconds, then opened them wide when the cloth leash dropped into her hand. With a tighter grip than necessary, Mariah, her knees shaking, knelt on the ground and outstretched the back of her hand for the dog to smell. The young canine took the invitation and actively sniffed her, blowing in and out as her nose perused Mariah's body like a human would a newspaper, her tail wagging a mile a minute.

"You like her?" Mike asked. He pointed to the wagging tail. "She likes you."

"She's a female?" Mariah stooped and checked her underbelly to verify. "Does she have a name?"

"Yes. Artemis, which means, in part, the Greek goddess of the hunt and chastity."

"Oh, a virgin." She turned to Cosmo. "You could change all that, buddy."

"Check out that doggy smile," John said with a chuckle as he petted Cosmo's head.

"Love at first sight. I'm sold." Mariah threw her arms around him. "You're the best." She kissed his head. "I'll move."

Chapter Nineteen

John had faced many dangerous situations in his life, but meeting Mariah's mother for the first time gave him the heebie-jeebies. He didn't know how much Mariah had revealed to her mother. Did she know he rolled around in a wheelchair? Would she care? Between his disability check from the government and his ample income from the ownership of a successful security business, he was financially set for life. A factoid he had not revealed to Mariah. Only his family was privy to the contents of his portfolio.

He glanced at Mariah sitting quietly in the passenger seat of his van as they wound through one of Fort Worth's middle-class neighborhoods where the residents took pride in maintaining their homes and keeping their lawns trimmed. Her mother still lived in the three-bedroom, two bath house where she grew up. He skimmed her face and smiled, envisioning her at ten years old, sporting blonde pigtails, cut-off jeans and tennis shoes. He imagined her as one hell of a competitor, handing the boys their lunch in a basketball game or even skateboarding. Whatever.

She appeared relaxed, with an arm resting on the window ledge, twirling her ponytail but he recognized the pretense. "What are you thinking about?" John asked, interrupting her musings.

"My mother and Franny meeting you."

"Franny will be there?" He gulped.

"Reinforcements." Mariah laughed.

"For whom, exactly?"

"Well, I don't need reinforcements. I'm on your side, babe. Besides, how scary could two little old grey-haired ladies be?"

"Very." He nodded his head emphatically. "I'm getting ganged up on." John slowed the speed while he gripped the steering wheel. "Cosmo, you've got my back, right?" When the dog whined and shoved his head under his blanket, John said, with a chuckle, "You're no help."

"They're preparing a nice garden brunch with all your favorites." She winked. "I got you covered. No cucumber sandwiches for my manly man." She rubbed a hand up and down his bicep.

John grew serious and sighed before he asked the obvious. "Does she know?"

"Know what?"

"Stop screwing around," he snapped. There was more edge in his voice than he intended. "You know what." He kept his tone flat and his voice low.

She pointed to his wheelchair. "If you mean that, I did mention it."

Certain his head was about to explode, John asked, "And?" He had planned to ask Kathleen for her blessing to marry Mariah but now, with Franny and lunch and God knows what other surprises, his nerves of steel had dissolved into a ball of fluttery uncertainty.

"And my mother can't wait to meet you."

When they pulled up to the curb next to the driveway of Kathleen's house, an elderly but spry female threw open the front screen door and bustled down the sidewalk toward them, wiping her hands on her apron as she approached.

Mariah waved to the woman, then unsnapped her seat belt and exited. "Where's Mom?"

John and Cosmo rounded the front bumper, catching the concern in Mariah's question.

"Is everything okay?" John asked.

The woman brushed loose grey strands of hair off her face. "She's in the kitchen." With a quiver in her voice, she added, "Cleaning up the mess."

With a nod toward John, she replied, "Yes, mostly."

"Mess?" Mariah started toward the house, then glanced over her shoulder at John and Cosmo, her face misshapen by a frown.

John stuck his hand out to the woman. "Hi, I'm John Armstrong." He pointed to the dog sitting at his side. "This is Cosmo. And you must be Franny."

She ignored John's outstretched hand, choosing instead to clutch him in a big hug. "That's me, family friend and Mariah's mother's 'bestie'." She squeezed his shoulders. "I've heard wonderful things about you." She stepped back, gazing at Cosmo. "You too, good boy."

She tilted her head and put her hands on her hips. "Apparently, I'm in the presence of a war hero."

A rush of heat flooded John's neck and face. "Thank you but I'm no hero."

"That's not what I've heard." She smiled.

"I'm just an ordinary guy in a wheelchair. Hero is way too difficult to live up to." Uncomfortable with the admiration, he changed the subject. "Now that introductions have been made, let's get that mess cleaned up."

Franny glanced at the house and then, in a concerned voice, said, "Before we go inside, I need to tell you something."

"What is it?" He sensed there was more to the mess than Franny originally told them.

"When I arrived this morning to help Kathleen with preparation for the brunch, I found a large shiny spot on the kitchen floor."

"Maybe Kathleen spilled something?"

"That's the thing. She wasn't up yet when I arrived, which is odd, but unless she spilled the liquid the night before and forgot to clean it up, the mess got there some other way."

Cameras. I need to check the cameras. "What was the liquid?" John asked.

"Weird. Water with a small amount of nearly invisible liquid soap. Just enough to make it dangerously slippery on the ceramic tile floor."

John's lips tightened into a thin line. "I can see Mariah's mother spilling some water and forgetting to clean it up based on what Mariah's told me about her dementia, but the soap on the tile floor adds a sinister dimension."

"I thought so too but didn't want to alarm Kathleen who was headed right for the spot when I stopped her."

"You did the right thing telling me first." He surveyed the street but viewed nothing unusual. "Why don't you go inside? I want to check out a few things out here."

"I'm glad you're here, John. I feel better knowing you're not going to brush this off. I don't think Kathleen should be alone and she's welcome to stay with me, but I don't know how much longer I'll be here. Please don't tell Kathleen but my kids are begging me to relocate to Arizona so I can spend more time with my grandkids." She hesitated. "And I'm seriously considering it."

"One thing at a time, Franny. I think you should be the one to tell Mariah's mom you're leaving whenever you feel the time is right."

Mariah stuck her head out the front door and shouted, "Y'all joining us?"

He waved and nodded. She shrugged her shoulders and disappeared inside.

"Lunch will be ready when you are," Franny said with a light squeeze on John's shoulder. She straightened her back and plastered a smile on her face as she turned toward the house. John realized she was attempting to put the best face on a hard decision, but he agreed it was probably the right decision.

The first camera on the side of the house was intact and appeared to be functioning. Hidden by a tree branch, it would be hard to detect. He rolled toward the back porch and jerked the wheels to a halt. The lens was spray-painted black. Whoever did this was in a hurry or had bad aim as the paint splattered on the aluminum gutter. *Got you!*

"There you are," Mariah called out to him.

He waved her over. "Check this out."

She peered up, following the direction of his finger, and exhaled an agonized gasp. "What happened?"

"I'd say who but it's the only one I've found tampered with so far. Problem is it's the one covering the back door and porch."

"Water with liquid soap was pooled on the kitchen floor, near the dishwasher. At first, I thought there was a leak in the machine, but Mom said she hadn't run it since Thursday. While we mopped it up, I questioned her like she was a suspect in a bank robbery." She wrapped her arms around her stomach and hung her head. "I accused her of spilling dishwater and forgetting to clean it up."

John's throat tightened at the pain he witnessed twisting her face when she lifted her head. "You didn't know. With the onset of her dementia—"

Mariah raised her hand. "Stop. Please. I thought we were past all this craziness. There's been nothing for weeks." She heaved a deep sigh. "Until now." She placed her hands on his shoulders. "Look, I know you're trying to help but I'm done doubting my mother. She assumed someone pushed her and I doubted her. I'm marching my ass back in there to apologize." With her shoulders squared, she did an about-face.

"Wait, Mariah, don't say anything to her about the camera. Let me retrieve my laptop and see if any of the other cameras captured the culprit."

Still facing the house, she fisted her palms and said, "She's in danger. I must warn her."

"No, don't. Not yet." John realized his plan to ask Kathleen for her blessing was already underwater. The day's priority, at least from his perspective, had gone sideways. "We need all the intel first."

"She needs protection," Mariah said through gritted teeth.

John sensed her frustration level was climbing and close to a boiling point. "We can stay here tonight. We're both armed, and Cosmo will alert us to any prowlers." John rubbed the K-9's chest, emanating an air of calm. "I do want you to discreetly find out if anything is missing."

Mariah nodded. "Good idea." She hesitated for a full minute before asking, "John, why would anyone want to hurt my mother?"

The answer was obvious from his vantage point, but he understood she had tunnel vision about wanting to ensure her mother's safety. "To make you vulnerable and more malleable, easier to control. To knock you off your signature firm footing."

"You're always the voice of reason." She smiled. "The funny thing is this asshole's plan isn't working. I'm more on my game than ever." After a quick kiss on the cheek, she continued, "Because of you."

"Glad I can help."

"Do you think we should file a police report?"

"And say what? We can't prove someone intentionally tried to harm your mother, only that a vandal spray-painted the camera." He noticed her furrowed brow. "If I find any hard evidence from the remaining cameras, we'll call the sheriff."

John eyed Franny and a woman, who could be Mariah's older sister, step out onto the screened porch. He offered a smile and a light wave after she beamed at him.

Franny waved them toward the porch. "Brunch is served. Come and get it."

Mariah waved John forward, and as he passed, she joked, "I caught that smile Mom gave you. Always a hit with the women."

"I think she was smiling at Cosmo."

"Yeah, right."

After John navigated the portable metal ramp positioned next to the stairs, he signaled Cosmo to wait on the porch.

"What's the meaning of this?" Kathleen asked as she squatted to pet Cosmo's head as John entered the house.

"Mom, this is John and that is Cosmo, John's service dog."

"Of course, John." She clasped both his hands in hers and held them tight. "Wonderful to finally meet you." She glanced at the dog and called out, "You too, Cosmo."

"Likewise, Mrs. Michaels."

"Please, call me Kathleen. Otherwise, you'll make me feel old."

"Oh, I wouldn't want to do that, ma'am, er, uh, Kathleen." He glanced at Cosmo sitting alertly on the other side of the door and said, "He's okay to wait for me outside." John slid back and forth in his chair, uncomfortable. Cosmo was rarely out of his sight.

"Nonsense. He goes where you go." Kathleen stepped to open the screen door. Cosmo dashed past the others and placed his head in John's lap. *Gosh, all the worry for nothing. I like her and all indications are it's mutual.*

He lost track of time as the women shared stories of their travel adventures, mostly cruises, and Kathleen showed John scrapbooks of Mariah growing up. She couldn't locate her daughter's high school yearbook, the one she most wanted to show John as it highlighted Mariah's academic accomplishments. She claimed it must have grown legs. The yearbook had always been kept on the bookshelf in Mariah's bedroom. John and

Mariah made eye contact and, after excusing herself, Mariah slipped away from the table and scurried into her bedroom.

The two older women delighted in the flirtatious banter with John so neither one of them noticed when Mariah disappeared for the better part of an hour. Caught up in a game of who could land the sexiest innuendo, they heaped on jokes about bananas in men's pockets until Cosmo begged to relieve himself.

Once outside, John whispered, "Thanks, buddy. Take your time. Pee on every bush."

While the canine explored the closest bushes, John finished checking the cameras. To his surprise, only one had been tampered with. Either the dirtbag didn't find the other cameras or he was in a blazing hurry. John wondered if one of the sheriff's patrols rolled by and scared him into faster action, entering the house. Wait. There were no signs of forced entry. The missing key. Did Mariah ever get the lock changed on the back door? His mind buzzed with possible scenarios until voices interrupted his musings. Franny was leaving. He checked his watch. How did it get to be five o'clock?

"So nice to meet you, John. I haven't had this much fun in quite a while." She winked at him and placed her finger on her lips indicating they'd both keep her secret about moving for now. He tilted his head in a slight nod.

Mariah joined the group, widening her eyes when only John could see her. *She found something.*

She hugged Franny, then turned to her mother. "Hey, would it be okay if we slept here tonight? It's a long drive back to the ranch and I'm tired."

"Of course, honey. I'd love the company."

"I need to get a few things from the van," John said, hoping Mariah would come with him.

"Need any help?"

Bingo. "Yes, thanks."

As they stepped out of earshot from Kathleen, John asked, "Did you ever get that lock changed on the back door?"

"Oh, crap. After Mom moved in with Franny…. I believed she was safe." She buried her face into her opened hands. "I meant to have a locksmith over and…. Ugh. No."

"Ever find the spare key?"

Mariah gasped. "No. At least *I* didn't. I was so sure Mom had misplaced it." She grabbed John's shoulders. "I checked and my yearbook *is* missing. I did the equivalent of a cavity search in the house. Nothing." She shoved her hands in her pockets. "We have to do something."

John opened the back door of his van and retrieved a power drill, which he handed to Mariah. He paused. "There is a possible different angle to this SNAFU."

"What are you thinking?"

"If whoever this was wanted to avoid a face-to-face with your mother while they snooped around her house, a little slip and fall might be a good early warning system."

Crimson covered her neck and flooded her face. "I'm gonna nail that psycho."

"I'll help you." He scrounged around in the toolbox until he located the equipment he'd brought to secure the ranch guest house.

"But first…." A security door chain hung from his hand. "I bought this to install as added security for your front door, but I'm going to mount it on your mother's back door tonight. Whoever is behind this hasn't broken any windows or jimmied any doors. They had a key."

Chapter Twenty

Mariah hadn't experienced that twisted, gut-wrenching stab in the pit of her stomach since she witnessed her father gut a pregnant female deer on a family hunting trip. Horrified but powerless to stop him at the age of ten, she swore between choked sobs, she'd prevent animal cruelty as an adult.

An emergency call logged in early while she and John were enjoying morning coffee with her mother. A young female deer caught in a hog trap overnight lay tangled in wire unable to free itself. Probably frightened out of her wits, it was a matter of time before the little girl mangled a leg trying to escape. She took a final gulp of coffee and banged the empty cup on the counter harder than she'd intended.

John jerked and fumbled his mug, spilling a few drops on the table. "What's up, babe?"

"Local yokels don't know how to properly build hog traps so deer can escape." She shoved her long blonde hair in a makeshift bun, then strapped on her gun belt. "I don't want to have to put down another animal due to hunter ignorance. Fingers crossed I can get there before the poor thing freaks out and breaks a limb."

"You're hot." John waggled his eyebrows. "I love the bun and gun combo."

"You need a cold shower." She bopped him on his

head, then winked. "Where's Mom?"

"She's on the back porch talking to Franny."

Mariah checked her watch. "Early visit?"

John fidgeted in his chair. "Franny is moving to Arizona at the insistence of her children."

"Way to lay it out there, dude." She rested her hands on her gun belt. "How does Franny feel about the move?"

"She's naturally torn but wants to spend more time with her grandchildren." He held out both of his opened palms. "She only told me yesterday and swore me to secrecy."

"Even from me?" Mariah tensed as she peered out the sliding glass door at Franny with her arms around her mother, who gripped a tissue in her fist.

"No, but with recent events, I figured it best to let the two ladies work it out."

"I get it." Despite last night's lack of kerfuffle with the motion detector lights remaining dark and Cosmo patrolling in his routine manner, the reappearance of her stalker was unnerving. She still had a job to do. A job she loved.

Mariah was backing up toward the porch door when a horn blew two sharp blasts. "Oh, crap. That's Tommy. I gotta go." She detoured onto the porch and hugged her mother, adding a light peck on the cheek. "See you soon, Mom."

She scooped up a pair of heavy-duty wire cutters she'd found in the garage earlier and paused by John on her way out the front door.

"Be here when I get back?" She stroked his hair with her free hand.

"Yep. Your mother and I are baking a loaf of

sourdough bread this morning while you're thrashing through the Texas underbrush saving wildlife."

His sense of humor was the first thing that hooked her, but, oh my God, he always had her back. She didn't know which attribute she loved more.

"You're my leaning post, John."

"Really?" He peered down at his legs lying motionless in the wheelchair and grinned. "Considering a leaning post absorbs shock and provides stability for the captain of a boat, are you calling yourself the captain of this boat?" He motioned with his hand encircling them both.

The emotion smacked her in her chest, like someone giving her CPR. His disability didn't limit his ability to love or care or be happy. She'd found a true partner, a real soul mate. Someone she could count on. She didn't always have to be in charge. He'd help carry the load.

"How about co-captains?" She winked.

"Done." His grin spread like sunshine across his face.

She couldn't believe her good fortune in being loved by a man like John Armstrong.

****

The rousing aroma of freshly baked sourdough bread permeated the kitchen and drifted through the house in a familiar bouquet. Memories of John's mother flooded his mind and reminded him of days gone by. Good times spent with her in the kitchen when she baked from scratch and handed him the spoon to lick, soothed his soul in a simple way.

"Need any help?" John asked as he rolled into the kitchen, inhaling a deep breath.

Kathleen pointed to the sourdough loaf on the nearby table. "You can slice."

She lifted a long, sharp knife from a wooden block, along with a cutting board, and positioned them on the kitchen table next to the cooled bread. "Coffee?"

Kathleen's warmth and ease around him instilled a welcomed sense of home. Her sensitivity and consideration of his condition didn't go unnoticed when she conveniently placed the cutting board and knife within his grasp. "Yes, black."

He sliced the loaf into thick pieces, cleaned the knife, and laid it on the counter.

"Tell me about your mother," Kathleen said as she filled an oversized mug with the hot, dark liquid.

Steam drifted past his nose and compelled him to inhale the combination of fruity and chocolate compounds. "Umm. One of my favorite smells." He smiled as he drew the mug toward his lips, then savored his first sip before speaking. "She deserved sainthood."

Kathleen buttered a slice of the newly baked loaf and handed it to John, meeting his gaze. "Mariah told me about what happened to your father. I'm so sorry for your loss."

"Thanks, but my mother got the brunt of the pain. He was the love of her life. She never remarried but devoted her life to ensuring my sister and I had a strong moral compass." He took another sip. "We didn't have an excess of material wealth, but we never doubted we were loved."

"It must have been hard as a boy growing up without a father." Kathleen placed her hand on his.

"I'd be lying if I said it didn't have its challenges but some of my father's Marine Corp buddies stepped up and acted as surrogate fathers. They made certain I comprehended…" —he scrunched up his nose and shrugged— "manhood." Single-fisted, he stuffed a chunk of the bread in his mouth, then made a prayer sign with his hands. "This is really great bread."

Kathleen beamed. "I'm so glad you like it." Then, out of the blue, she asked, "John, are you planning to marry my very independent daughter?"

"I'd like to."

"You have my blessing, dear."

"Thanks. That means a lot." *Problem solved.*

"You know how I know you're the one for my daughter?"

He shook his head. "Tell me."

"Mariah has always asserted to me she'd never marry but the way she accosts you with her smile…" She paused and fiddled with her apron. "All any mother wants is for her child to be happy." She swiped the corner of her eye. "You, my friend, do that in spades."

"Well, I'm glad you feel that way, Kathleen, and by the way, I love being accosted," he said with a hearty laugh.

His future mother-in-law giggled, then pecked his cheek with a kiss. "You and Mariah living here in Fort Worth, softens the blow of losing Franny." She heaved a deep sigh. "I won't be alone as this disease eats away at my independence."

"No, you won't be alone." He'd make certain of that, but he'd need Mariah's help working this problem. If only he'd understood the magnitude of the situation earlier. He wasn't even sure Mariah fully realized the level of her mother's mental deterioration until a few weeks ago. Franny had been an enabler of sorts, acting as driver, companion, and left brain for Kathleen. His heart ached. Mariah was the person this sweet woman loved most in the world, and he planned to take her away.

As she shuffled down the hall, Kathleen called out, "Nap time," and then disappeared into her room.

No way he could leave her behind. He'd work out a way to include her in his relocation plans.

****

Her mother was still asleep when Mariah arrived at the house later that afternoon. John had texted her inquiring when she'd be back within minutes of Tommy easing his truck up to the curb. *Good timing, bud.* Her partner declined her invitation to come inside saying he'd do clean-up allowing me more time with my squeeze, which was code for, he'd complete the needed paperwork from their afternoon deer rescue. Tommy liked to think he was hip.

She couldn't wait to see John and hear about his day with her mother and get a slice of her mother's yummy bread. The screen door swung open as she grabbed the handle.

"Well, hello, handsome." She stepped inside and while her eyes adjusted to the difference between the bright Texas sun and the single lamp lighting of the living room, with a deep breath, she inhaled his musk scent. "Somebody smells sexy."

He grasped her thigh and tugged her between his legs. His hands, fingers wide, slid up to her bottom and palmed both cheeks. She moaned as she grabbed his hair and guided his face into her groin. "My mother could mosey in at any second."

"Thanks for killing the moment," he mumbled and

rolled back.

"Still happy to see me?"

"Of course." He smiled, then reverted to his serious face. "We need to talk."

"Sounds ominous."

"It's not but it *is* important."

"Did my mother do something to make you doubt us?"

"Just the opposite. Kathleen's a total sweetheart. We talked enough for me to recognize that with Franny going to Arizona, your mom's going to need help, but Mike's ranch isn't the right choice for her. She needs the familiarity of her own home. Then, there is the problem of the stalker. We'll need additional security also."

"I have an idea, but we'll have to get Mom to agree."

"Let's hear it."

"While Tommy and I were out, he asked me to update him, and when I relayed the latest incident, he suggested I contact an old friend of ours, Alice Walker. She served in the Army as a medic, then joined law enforcement and worked as a deputy sheriff. We crossed paths frequently until she retired a year ago and started an in-home assisted care company for seniors. I reached out to her already and asked her if she'll personally take this one on and she said yes."

"Great solution, babe. I can replace the damaged camera and put in motion sensors, but I won't totally feel comfortable until this perp is caught."

"Understood. I did call a locksmith…finally." She tugged on her bottom lip with her teeth. "He can be out first thing tomorrow morning, but I have a mandatory staff meeting at eight a.m."

"Call him back. I got this. I'll grab Mike. Don't worry and stop beating yourself up. We'll have this place like Fort Knox."

Mariah leaned in and whispered against John's lips, "You're the best. You know that, right?"

"No, I'm very insecure," he said, peering at her with fluttering eyelashes. "You need to prove it to me."

With her hands threaded through John's thick, dark hair, she slipped her tongue past his lips and swept his mouth. He moaned and grabbed her breasts, massaging both nipples until the sweet throbbing between her legs made her forget where she was.

Chapter Twenty-One

Mariah wiggled back and forth in her chair, then crossed her arms, fighting the restlessness that had plagued her since the stalker invaded her life. The compulsive need to check her phone for updated texts from John or an emergency call from her mother drove her a little crazy but she'd live with the desire to be somewhere else until Alice, who graciously accepted her offer, was camped out at her mother's house. She rolled her chair back and, with a tug, opened her middle desk drawer where her source of comfort lay in a ribbon-tied stack. John's 'missing you already' cards, which she kept away from prying eyes by stashing them at the office, reminded her of what was important in her life. She clutched them to her heart and an air of calm descended her body.

"Hey, Mariah, staff meeting's starting. You coming?" Tommy peered at her from the door's edge.

"Sure." Heat crept up her neck as she dropped the cards in the drawer and closed it with a decisive shove.

"Was that a swoon?" He chuckled. "Is tough girl swooning?"

Mariah landed a punch on his arm as she passed him on her way into the hall. "I never swoon."

"Ha! Never say never, short stuff."

With a backward glance and exaggerated eye roll, Mariah strolled into the meeting room and took her seat.

The staff meeting, which usually lasted thirty minutes, droned on for more than an hour. Texas law enforcement was busy these days as the number of illegal border crossings exploded. In an unusual request, the governor ordered a contingent of game wardens to take a road trip to the border town of Brownsville and act in a support role to the understaffed Border Patrol. Game wardens from surrounding counties who opted to stay would cover their shifts. Law enforcement statewide was stretched thin.

Her boss revved up his intention as he spoke. "I'm asking for two volunteers to travel to Brownsville to assist our border patrol, who are overwhelmed, by the way, for a month-long rotation. I understand the hardship of being away from your families. I know it's a high-risk assignment, but the call has gone out from the governor's office to every county for two officers. That's the quota."

She glanced around the room. No hands shot up. He continued layering in a dose of guilt. "Since 1895, our Texas Game Wardens have played a critical role in protecting Texas. We're here to help the citizens of Texas and, if necessary, risk our lives to protect others."

An uncomfortable quiet settled over the room. Each jerk of the second hand on the large classroom clock resounded with a distinct tick. Mariah personally knew every game warden in Tarrant County. They were a tight group who not only worked together but partied together and shared celebrations and losses. There wasn't a person in the room not dedicated to the oath of their profession. But as Texas law enforcement, they were privy to the extreme danger and monumental level of cartel-driven criminality crossing the border. News the public were bombarded with, although alarming, didn't come close to revealing the perilous nature of border work. She glanced around the room. No one made eye contact except Tommy, who twirled his wedding ring in short jerks. The room was easy to read. They all shared the same concern. Family.

Frank cleared his throat. "Anybody?"

Wishing time would speed up, Mariah's hand crept up along her side and, as if on autopilot, stretched into the air. She kept her focus forward, but a pair of eyes drilled holes in the back of her head. A few strained seconds later, Tommy's deep voice resonated a "count me in." She whirled around in her chair and started to protest but Frank cut her off.

"See me after, Michaels."

Frank called an end to the meeting and waved Mariah forward. As she stood, a single clap started in the back of the room, followed by another until the entire unit was clapping as they exited the room. Tommy joined them and motioned for her to call him after the meeting with Frank.

"You don't have to do this, Mariah," he started.

"Don't I?"

"There are a lot of counties in Texas with a lot more resources than we have."

"You mean single officers?"

"No, I mean people who don't have what you've got going on in their lives. What about your mother? John?"

"Alice Walker, you remember her, has agreed to stay with my mother while I'm gone and until the threat is eliminated."

"That's good news. And John? Is he still here?"

"Yes, but his sister is due to give birth any day now and he'll head back to Florida." *At least I hope this motivates him to get home in time for the birth. Fingers crossed he sees it that way. Fingers double-crossed he isn't pissed about me springing this on him, but we probably won't leave for a few days, so he'll have time to adjust to the change.*

"Good thing Tommy volunteered to accompany you."

"Yeah, I appreciate the effort, but the credit goes to his better half who, in my opinion, is a model law enforcement wife."

"Agreed."

"By the way, what's the departure date?"

"Eight, tomorrow morning."

Mariah shrieked. "Did you say tomorrow morning?" She didn't wait for his answer but grabbed her backpack, bolted out the door, and ran headlong into Tommy's broad chest.

"Ouch," Tommy said, feigning bodily injury.

Mariah slapped his bulging bicep. "You shouldn't be lurking."

"How'd it go with Frank?" Tommy asked.

"I had to convince him I was up for the task."

"Did you?"

She nodded. "We leave at eight. Meet me at the office at seven to load the truck."

"Roger that. Go kiss your boyfriend goodbye. Oh, and since you won't get any sleep tonight, I'll drive."

As Mariah shoved through the exit doors to the garage, she raised her right arm and displayed her middle finger in a final salute.

****

"Am I ever going to be first in your life?" John said, barely concealing the anger bubbling beneath his stoic exterior. Cosmo, trained to sense signs of PTS in his master, nudged John's arm until he stroked the dog's head and back. The canine snugged close to John's chair and sat.

Mariah folded her arms and, in a low voice, said, "Frank asked for volunteers, but no one raised their hand. Not because they're cowards, John." She dropped her arms and inhaled a deep breath. "Tommy and I are the only team members who don't have children."

He could relate to dedication, to purpose, and most importantly to having your teammate's back. Sweat trickled down his neck as he imagined the scenario at the border. Did she fully understand the peril she was about to put herself square in the middle of? This assignment was more than ticketing some local yokel for not having a fishing license. Terrorists and drug smugglers crossed in the dead of night, ruthless, with nothing to lose if intercepted. Reports of women raped or kidnapped and sold into sex slavery by unsavory characters were rampant. Caught in a catch twenty-two of whether to back off and let her risk her life in a dangerous border zone or alienate her with an ultimatum not to go, resulted in a potential loss for him either way. Memories of his own combat engagements drove the need to change her mind about accepting the assignment.

"You didn't bother to check with me before you decided to raise your hand."

As soon as the words passed his lips, he realized

backing off would have been the correct move. Her face contorted into a deep frown.

"You act like we're already married." She fumed.

"Well, I want to be." He dug in his heels. "Don't you?" he said, his question as much a challenge as a need for an answer.

"I've never wanted to be married…." Her frown softened into a smile. "Until I met you."

"So, what's the problem?" He leaned forward in his chair, clasping her hands.

"I didn't expect we would tie the knot anytime soon." She gripped his palms. "We have a lot to work out, like where we live, my mother." Her voice trailed off. "Where is she, by the way?"

"Your friend, Alice, dropped by and when she noticed the commotion from the locksmith was rattling Kathleen, she spirited her off to the park."

"What a blessing she's turned out to be."

"Speaking of blessings, I asked your mother for hers and she gave it without hesitation."

"I didn't realize you had an old-fashioned streak." She smiled. "I'm glad she approved, as she should've."

"The other stuff is details. Once you get back from the border, we should have a heart-to-heart."

"So, you're okay with me going?"

"No, but I know better than to try and stop you. When's your departure?"

"Tomorrow at zero dark thirty."

"Better go pack and then get your fine ass back to Mike's and spend the night with me."

****

The traffic through Fort Worth trailed at a snail's pace. Mariah checked her watch and huffed. She'd spent the better part of the afternoon at her mother's house with John, Alice, and her mom, but after a lot of reassurance, everyone was on board with her assignment. She'd need to assure Tizzy she'd be back before the lease was up and offer to help pack and transport her belongings. As she rolled into the parking lot, she glanced around for Tizzy's car but didn't see it parked in her usual spot. The apartment was dark when she entered. She glanced at Tizzy's bedroom door left open. At work, no doubt. Mariah zipped into the bathroom and picked up the items she'd need. After dropping them into a cloth bag, she stuffed underwear, camo pants, and cotton t-shirts into her duffle bag. Three clean and pressed uniforms hung on her room door. She added those to the pile.

In a quandary whether to call Tizzy or leave her a note, she opted for the note. Tizzy was a PIA when it came to her need to know, especially regarding her whereabouts, and Mariah wasn't sure how much the State of Texas wanted to promote border security shortages. More importantly, Tizzy had gotten on her last nerve after she ambushed John. When she returned to the city, they'd have a face-to-face about that.

Her note simply said she was called to a different county to work for a month and named her return date. She signed the note and propped it next to Tizzy's favorite appliance, the coffeemaker.

****

Tizzy, elated from her afternoon of decorating her new digs, burst through the apartment door in an excited leap. She envisioned Mariah camped out on the sofa in an exhausted heap, a glass of wine in hand after a hard day in the field. Instead, shadows cast eerie patterns across the grey carpeted floor of the empty apartment. "Shucks." She glanced at the image on her phone. *I really wanted to share these pictures of my decorating genius with Mariah.* She stomped her foot and scattered several pieces of unopened mail that had been dropped through the mail slot. Without checking the address, she knew the letters belonged to Mariah. She changed her address to a post office box months ago. After flipping on the light switch, she bent to retrieve the items and perused the senders, gloating at the absence of John's routine, and totally stupid 'missing you' card before she placed the pile on the kitchen counter. *I obviously won my little war of words with the jarhead.*

A folded note, propped against the coffee maker, caught her eye. Her hand trembled in eager anticipation of reading the contents, hopeful it was an invitation to dinner or an apology for allowing John to be such an interloper, but expectation turned to despair as the words sunk in. Her jaw stiffened in a firm line as she crumpled the paper in her fist and threw it onto the floor. With her gaze fixed on the discarded note, her mind raged. *I'm not so easily dismissed, Miss Perfect. I've given you every opportunity to appreciate what I have to offer, afforded you the benefit of the doubt in your poor choice of men but you choose to belittle me with your lame excuses of work and schedule. I haven't even begun to show you what I'm capable of. The cost of you ignoring me will be the destruction of everything and everyone you love. First things first. If there was one camera in this apartment, there are others.*

After a meticulous search of the light fixtures, the wall hangings, and every nook and cranny in the apartment, Tizzy successfully located and disabled the six remaining cameras. Rather than simply unscrew the cameras from the wires, she tore them from the wall along with chunks of plaster, leaving gaping holes in the walls. She kicked a large piece of plaster across the room and laughed. "There goes the security deposit." With a defiant toss of her head, she sashayed into Mariah's bedroom.

Energized by anger and fueled by revenge, Tizzy ripped Mariah's clothes from their hangers and heaped them in a pile on the floor. With grim determination and a handy pair of scissors, she cut incisions into each piece until they were unrepairable. Pleased with herself, she progressed to the dresser where Mariah stashed her special occasion jewelry in a walnut jewelry box.

Her index finger posed thoughtfully on her chin. "Hmmm. I could use some new necklaces and matching earrings." She grabbed a tote bag from the top drawer and emptied each of the three small drawers into the opening.

Next, Tizzy turned to the supply of fashion accessories kept in a tray on the bedside table. She chose a pair of bronze aviator sunglasses, prized by Mariah, and with a dramatic flip of her wrist, let them fall to the floor. She crushed them with her boot. "Oh, whoops." She tossed her head back and laughed.

Stacking as many pairs of shoes as she could in the crook of her arm, she ran to the bathtub and withdrew a tube of gorilla glue from her pocket. Delighted at her creative efforts, she squirted the contents over the tops of the shoes, coating and securing them to the tub.

With a final satisfied glance around the apartment, she loaded one of Mariah's suitcases with the jewelry and the contents of her undergarment drawer. As she passed through the living room, she ran into the kitchen and grabbed the coffeemaker on her way out.

With one final task left, she skipped down the stairs and scanned the parking lot until she located Mariah's car. With her hands stuffed in her pockets, she sauntered to the back of the car. After a quick glance around, she squatted in front of the rear license and slid an air tag under the plate, then secured it with a drop of glue. Her only regret was having to wait an entire month for Mariah to discover her handiwork.

She loaded her car and glanced back at the apartment. Adrenaline surged through her veins as she reviewed the chaos she'd left behind. The deadness inside now replaced by the rapid thumping of her heart along with a rivulet of sweat escaping from her armpits excited her. But to achieve the full impact of the rush she craved, the heightened senses she so desired, she'd need to execute more revenge. *The clock's ticking. If I'm smart, I'll get my ass out of here now.* She slammed the trunk of her car and stared at the apartment key clutched in her hand. *No. I deserve more.*

Chapter Twenty-Two

Home for a week and he still hadn't mustered the nerve to discuss a potential move to Texas with his sister and brother-in-law. He practiced his speech on the drive home and lined up his reasons for relocating, number one being Mariah wouldn't leave Fort Worth, but stopped short after Gavin surprised him by installing a wooden ramp all the way from the hard-packed farm road to the top of this hillside perch. His throat tightened with emotion at this latest gesture from a man who expressed his feelings implicitly through his actions. Gavin clearly valued and assumed his permanence at the farm.

John scanned the acres of lush pasture below from the choice plot of Cross homestead Gavin had gifted him. Wildwood Farms was a tonic after his last trip to Texas and his home. He couldn't imagine living anywhere else. Cosmo perked up as two horses wandered into view, their tails flicking as they causally grazed the knee-high grass. This was also Cosmo's home, although if the dog could talk, he'd probably say home was with his master.

His gaze shifted to the wide porch attached to the main house. Gavin charged out the front door, waved his arms, then disappeared back into the house. Within a few seconds, he shoved through the screen door a second time and, after jumping off the three steps, set out in a fast jog toward, *uh oh, my cottage*. John left his phone at home despite the knowledge his sister was about to pop, thinking he could sneak away for an hour or so of rustic quiet. He sent Cosmo ahead to greet Gavin while he spun the wheels of his chair in rapid synchronized speed down the steep incline.

Gavin met him at the bottom, panting and out of breath. "Baby's coming. We're going. You in?"

"My sister's in labor?"

"Water broke and she's having strong contractions." Gavin hopped from one foot to the other. "Gotta get her to the hospital."

"Cosmo and I will hold the fort. You get going."

"Thanks, bro." Gavin spun on his heel and sprinted toward the house, arms and legs pumping in rhythmic power.

John studied Gavin as he disappeared, then eased the wheels of his chair into motion. "I'm going to be an uncle," he chuckled. "I'm going to be an uncle," he shouted, raising his fisted hands into the air.

****

"Was that 'lover boy' on the phone?" Tommy asked.

Mariah swung at her partner with a playful jab. "Yes, that was John. His sister had her baby, and he sounds smitten to his core."

"You sound surprised?"

She rubbed her brow. "I am, only because he's never expressed much interest in children or in becoming an uncle."

"You two haven't discussed the subject?"

"Nope." She shook her head. "In my defense, our relationship's been a little long-distance crazy. Not to

179

mention the stalker."

Tommy squeezed her shoulder. "Settle down. I'm not trying to give you a hard time." He glanced around at the immigrant encampment overflowing with tired, hungry people, most of whom didn't speak English and were promised a much different outcome by their coyotes. "This past week has been difficult enough."

Mariah followed his gaze. "Agreed."

"Have you talked about which side of the Mississippi you're going to live on?"

"Been broached but no decision in stone." She dragged her hands down her face. "Truth be told, I reckoned he'd come here. He can operate his business from anywhere. One of his best friends lives near Fort Worth and I have my mother. But now…." She propped her hand on her holstered gun.

"Give him some time, some sleepless nights, a few dirty diapers. He'll be packing."

"He texted me pictures holding the baby. They're bonded." She scrolled through her phone until she found the texted image and held it at eye level for Tommy to view.

"Whoa. He, I assume due to blue blankie, is a bruiser."

"Oh, stop." She laughed. "Yes, his name is Alexander and he's adorable."

"Big and adorable," Tommy added.

"You're obviously not ready for the parenting adventure," she quipped.

"Are you?"

"To be determined." She straightened her gun belt, dusted off her pants, and after another glance at John's picture, stuck her phone in her back pocket. "Our watch starts soon. Let's head over."

"Good avoidance technique," he said as he brushed by her.

****

Early mornings remained John's favorite time of day on the farm. Native birds welcomed the golden glow of the sun's bold arrival with full-throated cheering. He paused and bowed his head, experiencing the full audio impact of nature's chorus. Although the farm was a busy place, it was never a stressful place. There was always time to appreciate the special beauty of Wildwood Farms. He pictured Mariah next to him, hands intertwined, and sighed. He missed her.

The familiar reverberation of the barn's heavy doors, as they slid down the metal tracks, grabbed his attention. He checked his watch. Rob was right on time. Hired by Gavin's father as a barn manager a decade ago, he'd proven himself, with a few trial-by-fire challenges, as a trusted guardian over the multimillion-dollar residents inside those concrete walls. The Cross family treated him as one of their own.

Rob waved and pointed inside, signaling he was about to dispense the morning grain. The horses, also alerted by the activity, started nickering and, one by one, extended their curious faces over the stall doors. John waved Cosmo forward. Always the opportunist, the canine charged through the free-range chickens, dispersing them from their business-like pecking through the dew-covered grass in search of breakfast, circled back to him, then trotted into the barn.

"Morning, Mr. Armstrong," said Rob as he unhooked the first clipboard from the rounded peg next to the stall and passed it to John.

"Thanks, Rob, and you don't have to call me Mr. Armstrong."

"But you're a distinguished veteran. I do it out of respect."

"We've been over this," John said lightheartedly.

"Yes, sir, Mr. John." He saluted.

"John is fine." Not wanting things to be awkward, John saluted back before he began flipping through the pages on the chart, spending more time than necessary reading the overnight notes. One of the duties his sister had assigned him while she recovered from childbirth involved reviewing the charts of the horses from the night before, paying special attention to any equine on a treatment plan or meds. Any changes were noted. He also eyeballed each one for general disposition before they were released into the lush pastures behind the barn. Rob could easily do this task in Ariel's absence, but she insisted he be her temporary set of eyes. Cool. He'd wade through six barns for the better part of the morning if it kept his mind off Mariah.

With the report from this morning tucked under his arm, John ascended the ramp connected to the front porch of the main house, a big smile plastered on his face.

"Hey, sis, how's my nephew?" He bent toward the bundle in the crook of Ariel's arm while redirecting Cosmo's inquiring nose away from the baby.

Ariel drew back the blue blanket enough so the infant's head and face showed.

"Asleep," she said in a whispered tone. "How'd it go with Rob this morning?"

John kept his gaze locked on the tiny body. "He keeps calling me Mr. Armstrong despite my insistence he not. Says it's respect for my service."

"We're all proud of you, my sweet brother." Her voice wavered.

He understood her emotion. If he glanced up, there'd be the familiar sadness in her eyes. Grief from the reminder of the misfortunes of war. Loss she suffered because of their father's and his military service. She tried but failed to hide the pain when she expressed her pride in their sacrifice. His throat tightened and he swallowed hard. *Not today*. He kept his gaze averted and strengthened his resolve not to cave while he figured out what to say to lighten the mood.

"It's been two weeks since Elmo's birth." He glanced up as she swiped at a tear. "I'll bet you and Gavin can count the hours of sleep you've both had on one hand."

"Alexander." She wagged her finger at him and smiled. "An exaggeration but definitely short on sleep." She suppressed a yawn.

"Let me have a whack at the next all-nighter with *Alexander*," he said, over-pronouncing the given name but happy the Elmo nickname had created the mood shift he wanted.

"You mean tonight?" She stifled a laugh. "Thanks, but I'm up to nurse every two hours." She snugged the blanket around the baby's shoulders. "Hey, how's Mariah? You guys good?"

"Yeah. She'll be returning from the border in a week or two."

"Will you be heading back?"

"Depends." He shrugged.

"On what?"

"On whether or not I'm needed here."

"Little brother, you're always wanted here but I think you've more than fulfilled the need. You have your own life to live. Better get to it."

The bundle in Ariel's arms shifted. Two tiny, fisted hands escaped the blanket. "Somebody's awake," John said as he peeked at his nephew's face screwed up into a frown, legs flailing.

"Hey, buddy." John turned to his sister and asked, "How you know what he wants?"

Ariel unbuttoned her shirt halfway down and nodded to Alexander's head as it bobbed back and forth. "That's the boob bob."

"Oh god. Time for me to go to work." John shielded his eyes as he headed for the door.

"Have fun," Ariel responded with a chuckle.

"You too." He glanced back as Alexander locked onto his sister's breast. A fluid warmth, like liquid sunshine, filled his senses. Family would always be number one in his life, but he wondered if he'd ever have his own Elmo. The better question was, could he? What if Mariah wanted a child and he couldn't give her one? *Bummer, but first things first. I need to get back to Texas and pop the big question.*

****

John rolled up to his desk and turned on his monitors, anxious to check up on Tizzy. From the first time he laid eyes on her, combined with a few musings from Mariah about her behavior, he'd been wary. But after the recent dinner where she showed her true and very dark colors, he was determined to get Mariah away from her and if not to Ocala, then out to Mike's ranch. His own sense of the situation was Mariah had gone overboard giving Tisdale the benefit of the doubt partly because Mariah was good that way and partly because her life demanded so much of her attention, she didn't assign enough of it to her own well-being. He'd arrive back in Texas in a week armed with articles by experts about narcissism. She didn't have to believe him. He'd also researched techniques on handling manipulative people and come across a strategy called, "grey rocking." He couldn't wait to give it a test run.

The file labeled Mariah's apartment opened and he clicked on camera number one. After entering today's date, he waited for an image to pop up, but seconds passed, and the screen remained dark. Working methodically, he checked his physical connections first. As he worked through the process, confirming each link, his heart thudded against his chest. *What's going on with this camera?* Next, he confirmed his live network by switching to the folder labeled Kathleen's House. A perfect view of his future mother-in-law's backyard and garden appeared. He switched to the next camera in the file and blew out a breath when he viewed Kathleen, appearing relaxed, sitting next to her new caregiver on the porch. Maybe there was a glitch with camera one at Mariah's apartment. He hovered the mouse over camera two in Mariah's bedroom and clicked. *Dark.* He rewound and a few seconds passed before a picture showed on the screen. He hit pause. A figure appeared in the doorway. He leaned in to get a better view. A female lifted her head and peered around the room. Then, a close-up image of Tizzy's face appeared. *I can't believe it. She's gloating right into the camera.* He paused the feed and checked the time stamp in the corner of the screen. *That's the same day Mariah left for the border.* He zeroed in on the top she was wearing. *What the hell? Is that one of Mariah's uniform shirts?* As he shook his head in disbelief, her hand raised over the lens. The video died. *Son of a bitch! Tizzy found the cameras. Did she find them all?*

He continued to check every camera in Mariah's apartment with the established timeline. A chill raced up his spine as he arrived at the only logical conclusion. The cameras had all been discovered and disabled the day Mariah left for the border. Tizzy had lost it.

John grabbed his cell phone and dialed Mike. Straight to voice mail. He left the message, *"A storm's brewing. Where are you, man?"* His next call was to Gavin, who after hearing what he'd discovered and after a string of four-letter words, agreed John needed to return to Texas, get back up from Mike and possibly local law enforcement. As far as Ariel was concerned, John's sudden departure would be explained as a horny dude who couldn't wait another minute to see his woman. Gavin ruled as his wingman.

Experience from being a Marine enabled John to ease into a state of readiness. His duffle bag, stuffed with t-shirts, underwear, and toiletries was ready to go at a moment's notice. He added a few pairs of pants, his weapon and ammo, then zipped it shut.

"Cosmo, get packed. We're headed back to Texas." Cosmo responded by gripping his food bowl in his teeth and dropping it in a large tote bag labeled, Cosmo, already filled with food and bottles of water.

Chapter Twenty-Three

In past trips to Texas, John took advantage of his cruise control and hummed down the interstate in happy anticipation of throwing his arms around the hot woman waiting at the end. While his enhanced stereo speakers blared rock music, he'd drum his fingers on the steering wheel. Today, he gripped the living crap out of that wheel. Stress dictated his constant creep over the speed limit as his mind wandered in hypnotic circles, trying to make sense of why Tizzy disabled the cameras. What was she up to? What did she want? His gut flip-flopped in the familiar signal of danger close. He'd refined his ability to listen to his gut while in Afghanistan and it had kept him alive. He glanced at the speedometer edging over seventy, but his urgency to reach Fort Worth before Mariah arrived home into a possible ambush, intensified. *Screw it.* He floored the accelerator. The scenery blurred as he closed the distance between the Texas border and Tizzy's worst nightmare.

Mike called as John entered the outskirts of Dallas. His lack of surprise at John's revelation about the cameras confirmed he was of the same mind about Tizzy, and he was all-in on tackling the problem.

"ETA to the apartment complex?" John asked.

"I can be there in an hour. I'll supply my special tools." Mike chuckled.

"Good. I don't have a key." John huffed. "Or working legs to climb those stairs."

"No worries, brother. I got you." Mike disconnected the call.

John arrived at the apartment complex first and cruised the parking lot for Tizzy's MINI. After confirming her car was not in its usual spot, he parked in a parking space within view of Mariah's apartment and the entry gate to the complex. *Only one way in and one way out. Good overwatch security while Mike works his magic.*

John's phone beeped indicating a text message had arrived. He cast a brief glance to the screen assuming it was Mike alerting him to his arrival but was surprised when red heart emojis flooded the text box followed by, —*See you tomorrow, big guy.*—

In his many long-distance conversations with Mariah, since he uncovered the anomaly with her roommate, he never revealed his discovery. She had enough on her plate without the added stress of worrying about 'Tizzy gone bonkers'. Besides, there was nothing either of them could do about the situation until they returned to Fort Worth. He did text her back he'd arrived a few days early with the excuse Mike needed help at his ranch. Not a total lie. Mike was shorthanded. He weighed the consequences of withholding the truth from her against protecting her at all costs. Protection won, hands down.

Cosmo alerted to the parking lot gate with his usual whimper and intense focus anytime Mike arrived. John shifted his gaze from his phone to Mike as he entered the code Mariah had given them and eased through the gate. John waved his arm out the window motioning him over. Mike backed his truck next to John's so the two driver's windows aligned.

"Hey, buddy. You ready for this?" Mike asked. His arm rested casually on the open window ledge.

"Let the games begin," John said. "Cosmo and I will do overwatch and text you if company arrives." Cosmo edged past John, balanced on his hind legs, and popped his head out the open window.

With a soft chuckle, Mike stuck his hand through John's window and rubbed the dog's head. "Good boy, Cosmo." He then exited his truck and slung a black duffle bag over his shoulder. After winking at John, he patted the side a few times and, with a brisk stride, advanced toward the second-floor apartment.

John surveyed the area with his head on a constant swivel after Mike disappeared through the door of the apartment. Minutes passed before John's phone rang.

"That was fast," John said.

"Bro. I'm glad you're sitting down. This is some crazy-assed, warped behavior."

"Are the cameras disconnected?"

"Uh, disconnected? The bitch destroyed them along with the apartment."

John shook his head. "She's a raging lunatic!"

Frustration at not being able to jump out of his van and sprint up the stairs to view the scene for himself seized his mind. How could he assess? Devise a plan of action? He pounded on the steering wheel and struggled to clear his head. He needed a sit rep. "Get back out here. I've got a GoPro mounted on a helmet with a Bluetooth connection. We can work up the damage assessment together."

"It's not pretty, man."

"Just do it." John's upper body shuddered. "I'm going to contact the manager and have him come up."

John fought to tamp down his anger toward Tizzy while he did an online search for the main number for the apartment complex. The last thing Mariah needed after a month-long beat down of Texas heat and dry dust was this SNAFU.

The back door of his van swung open, and Mike thrust his head in. Cosmo leapt to the rear, greeting the man with excited yelps. With one hand rubbing Cosmo's head, Mike rummaged through the boxes until he located the camera equipment. John signaled Mike he was on the phone with the manager.

"Thanks. My friend, Mike, will meet you at apartment 2012B." John nodded to Mike as he spoke, "Yes, he's on his way now."

Mike shut the back door and as he strolled past the driver's window, helmet mounted, gave John a thumbs-up.

John observed Mike and the manager greet each other and as they entered the apartment, the manager held his phone in a vertical position, no doubt to capture Tizzy's psychotic break. *Good. None of this is on Mariah.*

The first view of the apartment had John gasping. What little furniture remained was stacked in the middle of the living room like she planned to build a bonfire and burn it all down. Mike zeroed the GoPro in on the opposite wall where red paint splattered the message, "Ignore This Bitch." Heat spread up his neck and face. Tizzy would pay for this. He'd make sure of it. If he had his way she'd be put down like a rabid dog.

He grimaced at the prospect of how much damage

would be in Mariah's bedroom but spoke to Mike through the two-way earbud. "Check out her bedroom."

"You sure?"

"Just do it, man. I want to see if any of her stuff is missing."

"Copy that."

A few minutes seemed like hours before the GoPro displayed a more dark reality of Tizzy's unchecked rage. Mariah's prized aviator sunglasses lay in pieces on the floor. They'd be the first thing he bought for her after this piece of trash was caught and punished. The camera swung to view the empty jewelry trays tossed on the floor next to the glasses. John spewed aloud a string of four-letter words until Mike interrupted him.

"I get it, bro. Acts worthy of word vomit."

"Good thing you can't read my mind."

"Seen enough?"

"Could it get any worse?"

"Well, shoes glued together in the bathtub, depending on what woman you talk to, might qualify."

John grunted. "Anything worth salvaging?"

"Don't think so. There might be one coffee cup that didn't break when the little witch played destruction derby with the dinnerware."

"I've seen enough. Make sure the manager calls the sheriff. I'm going to call Frank and give him a heads-up. Tizzy's coming for Mariah."

Chapter Twenty-Four

The manager had turned over all the evidence to law enforcement and was in the process of cleaning up the damage, but John didn't want his love's homecoming to be ruined. His gut told him Tizzy's extreme narcissism wouldn't allow her to walk away. He rechecked the security cameras he'd strategically placed around the guest house on Mike's farm and was headed toward the main house when his phone dinged with a text notification. He smiled. It was from Mariah. An attached image of her wearing her mud-splattered work boots, her clothes covered in road dust, and her trademark ponytail sent sparks of pleasure surging through his body. Maybe wishful thinking or phantom sensation but he'd bet money she excited feelings in his lower limbs. Her message read, —*Been way too long. Headed back with Tommy. In your loving arms tomorrow. Cause you're fire, caliente, hotter than hot sauce.*—

His stomach flipped. Mariah's homecoming would be bittersweet due to the storm brewing on the horizon. He'd worked the problem with Mike on how to postpone Mariah's discovery, at least until she'd caught up on sleep, but at some point, he'd have to tell her she'd lost most of her worldly possessions. Then came the hard part. Navigating the aftermath. Whatever her reaction, he'd deal.

—Can't wait. Don't waste time going to your apartment. I picked up a change of clothes and toiletries for you. Hi to Tommy.— John swallowed a twinge of guilt as he sent the reply. A small white lie as he never said where he picked up the items.

She replied with heart emojis. *—Mike forwarded pictures of Artemis to my phone with tags that read, "Hooman, I missed you." Also, "Come home. I need a head scratch." Making a beeline for Mike's ranch.—*

—I'll be waiting.— Hmmm. She didn't mention days off.

He'd conspired with Frank to award her three days off with the real intention of keeping her safe. *—Have you checked in with Frank?—*

—Oh yeah. Almost forgot. Three days off, babe.—

He muttered, "Good man, Frank." Then replied, *—I know how we can fill those days.—*

A laughing woman meme appeared on his screen, then the words, *—I'm picturing you twirling your mustache like one of those villains from a silent movie. LOL.—*

—Don't have a mustache.— His heart swelled. He loved the banter with her. She made him whole. *—Will grow one if it turns you on.—*

****

After a month spent in the sweltering heat at the border town of Brownsville, engaged in assisting border patrol with processing illegals crossing the border, Mariah breathed a sigh of relief at Frank's order for her to immediately take those days off. Her fair skin was sunburned, her feet had blisters, and she was exhausted. The past month had her reassessing her career goals. She'd joined the game warden community for the protection of animals, not pursuing clever coyotes and dangerous drug couriers through the Texas chaparral. She glanced at Tommy, who had insisted on driving her out to the ranch, and decided not to mention her doubts to him. She'd be in a better head space to tackle that conversation after spending a few days chilling with John and Cosmo and bonding with Artemis.

As the turnoff for the expressway toward Mike's ranch approached, Tommy maneuvered to the far-right exit lane but at the last minute, she asked him to take her to her apartment. He swerved back into the center lane.

With a raised eyebrow, he asked, "Why?"

"I realize I'll need my truck."

She trusted Tommy, but he used any excuse to rile her up and he'd see this side-trip as a reason to tease her because she wasn't moving at break-neck speed to see her hottie boyfriend. But truth be told, Tizzy had texted her during her absence, offering her support and asking her how things were going with her assignment, and even surprisingly asked about John. Had he returned to Florida? How were things going between them? Mariah hadn't bothered to mention her roommate's texts to John as she understood his animus toward Tizzy. The last message she received from her soon-to-be ex-roommate said there was a surprise waiting at their apartment and she couldn't wait to share it. A quick stop wasn't going to rain on John's parade. She owed Tizzy that much. She'd make it fast.

"I doubt that you'll be going anywhere but the bedroom, bathroom, and maybe the kitchen for the next few days."

"Y'all are funny." She slapped him on the arm,

relieved she was finally home.

As Tommy passed through the entry gate, she spotted her SUV parked right where she'd left it. "Over there." She pointed to the second row of vehicles.

While Tommy wheeled the official truck to the right and slowly rolled to his partner's familiar ride, Mariah collected her belongings. She peered at the apartment where she'd spent the last eighteen months, reminded of all the life-changing events she'd experienced. John was at the center of the change in her life. She hopped out of Tommy's truck, said goodbye, and started toward the building. She cast around the parking lot for Tizzy's car but didn't see it. Then checked her watch. Rush hour traffic would start to build very soon, adding minutes, maybe an hour to her arrival time at the ranch. She sent a quick text to Tizzy saying she'd arrived home and explained she would come by the next day to help her with any last-minute packing and pick up her surprise. She stuffed her phone in her back pocket and climbed into her truck. As she drove out of the parking lot, the anticipation of a peaceful evening along with a temporary respite at Mike's place soothed her tired body and jagged nerves. Sometimes being apart from someone taught you just how much they meant to you. If John asked her to marry him, she'd say, 'hell yes'. With her total focus on arriving at the farm, she didn't notice the black MINI Cooper tucked in traffic a few cars behind her.

****

The lights from the skyscraper windows faded as Mariah left the city limits. The beltway became a two-lane country road with only a rising moon and occasional headlights illuminating the way forward.

Her stomach growled, reminding her she hadn't eaten since morning when she and Tommy stopped at Waffle King for breakfast. John had promised a ribeye steak and all the fixings when she arrived at Mike's, tempting her to drive faster than the posted speed. She glanced in her rear-view and, except for the reflector stubs demarcating the center of the road, the night was pitch black on an empty road. She rolled down the window, turned up the radio volume and belted out the words to a familiar tune. Despite the physical annoyance of aching muscles, sleep-deprivation, and gnawing hunger, Mariah's spirit soared. Her future was filled with promise. Life was good.

As she approached the last wide bend in the road before Mike's turnoff, a pair of headlights joined her on the empty highway. She put on her turn signal and slowed. The car behind her mimicked her action, maintaining the distance between them. Mariah glanced in the rear-view and mumbled, "Safe driver?"

Her tires comfortably entered the dual ruts of the hard-packed dirt road and rolled forward at the speed of going through a car wash while she texted John an ETA of five minutes followed by three heart emojis. A flare of red caught her eye as the brake lights of the passing car flashed. She turned to view the car slow down until it was perpendicular to the farm's entrance, then speed away. She shook her head. *Are you lost?*

While her car continued to slow roll down the road, she kept one hand on the steering wheel, and rummaged in the top pocket of her backpack until she grasped a familiar cylinder-shaped object. She flipped on the overhead light and carefully followed the outline of her full lips with the soft pink lipstick. Then, with a quick tug, she freed her long hair from the elastic band, which normally kept her natural blonde locks snugged back in a tight ponytail. She shook her hair, using her fingers to fluff the sides. Next, she unbuttoned the top two buttons on her shirt, so the ample cleavage prevailed. Was the message too obvious? She didn't care. She wanted him.

From out of the darkness, a bright light bounced toward her. This far out in the country, there weren't any streetlights. But you could see the stars. She smiled at the prospect of star gazing with John on the back porch of the guest house. The outline of two dogs trotting toward her entered the cone of light from her car's headlights. *Cosmo and Artem*is. *John won't be far behind.*

Mariah held the down button of her front windows and leaned her head out. "Hello." The dogs raced up to her door, wagging their tails and barking.

She exited and kneeled, grabbing both dogs by the neck for hugs. "You're so beautiful."

"I've never been called beautiful before," John called out as he rolled up next to her in a modified ATV.

"Nice wheels." Mariah's grin stretched across her face. She leaned over and grabbed his cheeks then tugged them toward her until she was nose to nose. After engaging in an Eskimo kiss, she joined her mouth with his, parting her lips in invitation. John obliged and groaned when their tongues intertwined in an aroused dance. Her hunger for him exploded, but when she cupped his crotch, he broke the embrace and leaned back.

"What a Texas welcome," he said with a tremble in his voice while he pointed to the bulge in his pants. "I really missed you."

"I have a cure for that." She tilted her head in the direction of his erection. "Maybe we should double-time it to the house."

With his index finger, he traced her lips. "I'm happy you're back."

"Good to be home." The words hung in the air. *Home*.

Chapter Twenty-Five

John barely tasted his food as he ate, staring at the hot babe across the table. *She chose me?* Tonight, he'd propose to the woman of his dreams. Based on Mariah's level of passion earlier when they'd arrived at the guest house, he was confident he'd get a 'yes'. But her fevered murmurs of sex lasting forever sealed the deal. He'd give her a candied apple forever.

They hadn't agreed on whose side of the Mississippi they'd live but when he asked her if she could picture herself atop a hillside, gazing out on acres of emerald pastures dotted with million-dollar horse flesh, she climbed on top of him and pumped out round two.

He hadn't wanted to spoil the evening with the bad news about Tizzy, but he wanted it to come from him. It was only a matter of time until her phone buzzed and either the police, her boss, or the apartment manager crapped all over their night.

"That steak was delicious." She shook the napkin from her lap and patted the corners of her mouth. "I don't think I ever want to see another Taco."

"Noted."

"It's good to see you, John." She stretched her arm across the table, her palm open.

He squeezed her hand. "There's something I've been wanting to ask you."

"Yes."

"You don't know what I'm going to say."

"Oh, but I do and it's unequivocally yes."

"Unequivocally? Nice." *I should quit while I'm ahead but…* "Your mother told me you never planned to marry."

"True but that was before I met you." Her eyes glistened with moisture but stayed locked on his face.

With his free hand, John retrieved a small velvet case from his pants pocket and drew back the top. He'd convinced Kathleen to help him select the ring. The surprised gasp Mariah uttered when she viewed the contents, conveyed he'd nailed the choice. He nodded toward her left hand.

Her fingers trembled as she extended her hand. "John, this is too much."

"Nothing is too much for you," he said as he slid the two-carat yellow diamond over her ring finger.

Mariah splayed her fingers out and rotated her hand, so the light bounced off the princess cut facets. "It's flawless."

"That's what the salesman said." He winked at her, feeling satisfied he'd scored.

"How did you know about the yellow preference?"

"You're the yellow rose of Texas, right?"

With her hand perched on her hip, she scowled at him. "Y'all better fess up."

"Okay, okay. Your mother helped me," he confessed.

"It appears my mother is not as addle-brained as I assumed." She chuckled. "When I was a little girl, I played dress-up and told her I wanted a yellow diamond engagement ring because I was the yellow rose of

Texas."

"Her long-term memory is excellent. She told me that story while we were shopping for the ideal ring. We had a lot of fun picking it out."

"Well, it's perfect." She leaned in and kissed him on the cheek. "But I know this set you back and I would have been happy with something less expensive."

"I only plan to get married once."

"I hope you didn't go into debt for me."

"No." He hesitated to get into his portfolio at this moment. He wanted to wait until the big, 'where are we going to live,' question was addressed. If she understood how successful his business was, how many years it had taken him to build the clientele in Florida, it might help convince her to lean his way.

"I paid cash."

"Wait a minute. Did you say, cash?" She surveyed the ring up close.

He laughed. "It's real, babe."

"Is the surveillance business that lucrative?"

"It has been for me." His comfort level with admitting he was a millionaire clawed at him like fingernails on a chalkboard. He'd always planned to be a career military guy. Money was never his motivation, but he'd stumbled onto a niche with knowledge he'd gained as a Marine doing intelligence work overseas. Now, the entire Ocala horse racing industry depended on him for security. Her expression shifted from surprise through shock to amusement before she spoke.

"I assumed you told me everything, John." She eased herself onto his lap and swung her arm around his neck. "But you've been holding out on me." She flattened her forehead to his.

"No, I haven't." He inhaled the fresh peppermint scent of her lip gloss and wanted to dip his tongue in her mouth but continued, "Never seemed to be the right time."

"If there's anything else you want to tell me, now would be good." She twirled the ring on her finger.

And there it was. Although her tone was lighthearted, he'd better tell her about Tizzy pronto or risk serious damage to the trust in their relationship.

****

Mariah's heart told her, even sang to her, that she could trust John. He was straight-up the most honest, no BS guy she'd ever met and the only kind of man she'd ever marry even if it meant conceding Ocala would become home sweet home.

"My feelings for you are real and not motivated by financial gain. You know that, right?"

"I do." He rubbed her back in light, circular strokes. "There is one more thing I need to read you in on."

The serious tone in John's voice forewarned her of bad news. "The stalker?" she asked.

"Yes." He retrieved a notebook computer from the side table next to them.

His brow furrowed deeper and deeper as he scrolled through the files. As he clicked on one labeled Tizzy, his jaw pulsed in a tight clinch.

"John, what's going on?"

"Just watch." He tapped the play arrow.

She did watch…in horror…as her former roommate performed demolition derby on her apartment. The profound rage expressed in Tizzy's message scrawled in red paint on the wall, shocked and confused her. The word, 'bitch' stung. In the year they shared the living quarters, she'd never experienced this aspect of Tizzy's personality. Had there been signs? Did she miss them? She searched her memory. The dysfunction, apparent and extreme now had been well hidden behind a pretended shyness and insecurity. Bottom line, she'd been too distracted by her job, her mother and John to notice what was happening in her own house.

The view swung into her bedroom and zeroed in on the crushed sunglasses. She gasped. "My aviators!"

John laid his hand on her head. "I've already ordered you a new pair."

Mariah murmured a thank you before returning her attention to the next scene as Mike focused the camera on the bathtub.

"She poured glue on my shoes?" She dropped her head into her hands. "They're all ruined," she said between sobs.

"There's more."

"I've seen enough." Mariah choked out the words as she withdrew her arm and swung her leg out of John's lap. She tried to stand but her knees wobbled, and she sagged into John's chair arm. "Turn it off."

John grabbed her wrists and tried to steady her, but she rebuffed him, exhaling short bursts of air. "I need to get control of this situation. I need to call the police."

"I've notified your apartment manager and Fred. The manager filed a police report. There's already a BOLO out on her."

"I'm so sorry, baby. You tried to warn me."

"Nothing to apologize for."

"But I dragged you into this insane drama and now

you're cleaning up my mess."

"We're in a partnership and that's in the job description."

"Why me, John? What did I do to deserve this?"

"Nothing. You're a good person, Mariah. And she's a wacko. The fact you see the good in others isn't a flaw."

"I feel bad I didn't believe you and I feel even worse I justified Tizzy's behavior as quirky and eccentric rather than seeing her true character."

"She's a classic narcissist. Her behavior appeared normal because she believed she was the focus of your attention. When I entered the scene, it triggered her."

Mariah froze. "My mother. I was so intent on seeing you, I didn't check in. What if Tizzy goes after her?"

"She's safe. Mike and I checked her cameras. They haven't been disturbed. Alice notified law enforcement and is with her. Your mother is blissfully unaware of anything wrong."

"I really need to process everything that's happened."

"It all leads back to Tizzy. The false 911 calls, Tommy's accident, break in at your mother's house."

Mariah grabbed her chest. "Good God. She texted me she had a surprise for me when I got home but I didn't go in the apartment."

"You're safe here. She has no connection to Mike and this place is off the grid."

****

Mariah, her head propped in her hands, stared out the window with a fixed gaze. She hadn't said much since he'd spilled the beans about her roommate being a psycho.

John had underestimated how much the news would throw Mariah off her game. He didn't enjoy being the bearer of bad tidings, but did he really have a choice? When she told him she almost entered the apartment to accept Tizzy's surprise, the prospect of what could have happened shook him to the core. For her own safety, she had to be informed of what she was dealing with. Once Tizzy was apprehended, she'd get closure and life would return to normal. They'd put this crazy episode behind them.

"Hey, babe, you want a glass of wine to go with those deep musings?" *A little humor might help.*

"Sounds good."

"No wisecrack back and her lips barely parted but at least she responded," he said.

"Hmmmm," she murmured.

He poured her a generous glass of wine and positioned it in front of her. "Your favorite, Riesling." Her hand shot out, encircling the stem, and she lifted the glass to her lips, gulping a healthy slug of wine. She paused briefly then repeated the swallow.

"I like your style. Lift, slug, repeat, lift, slug, repeat."

That got a response but not the one he hoped for. She began to whimper, her chest heaving with sobs as a torrent of tears cascaded down her face, dripping from her chin before wetting her shirt. Artemis, who had been sleeping in a tight curl by the door, lifted her head and tilted right, then left at the odd sound emanating from her new mistress. John gave a hand signal for her to go to Mariah as he crept forward to the table where she sat, hunched over and miserable. Artemis arrived first and nudged Mariah's leg. When there was no response, she laid her head in Mariah's lap.

"Thanks, girl," Mariah said through choked sobs. She stroked the dog's large head.

John tucked in close to his lover's chair. "You okay?" He understood she wasn't, yet he was at a loss for words.

"No, but what I am is angry, confused, sad, and most of all ashamed." She sniffled.

"I understand all those emotions, but you have nothing to be ashamed about. Tizzy's the one who should be ashamed."

"I should have read her better and because I failed, I put the people I love the most at risk."

"Nonsense. We're all fine."

"Tizzy is still out there planning god knows what."

"Mariah, she's aware the cameras recorded her trashing the apartment and she knows we're on to her. My bet is she's halfway to Canada by now."

John's words of encouragement were interrupted by the ding of an incoming text. —Hey, bro, running late from picking up the K-9 in Houston. Feed the dogs in the kennel for me?—

John replied with a simple thumb's up emoji.

"What's up?"

"O'Malley needs me to feed the dogs in the kennel. He's running late."

"You want me to come with you?"

"Always, but I won't be long. He's only got three dogs in training right now. Why don't you take a hot bath while Cosmo and I dish out the kibble. When I get back we'll snuggle in front of the fireplace. Just the four of us."

"Deal."

Her smile settled him. Besides, the few minutes alone would give him time to check with Fred and the local sheriff to get an update on Tizzy's whereabouts.

Chapter Twenty-Six

She was in luck. John was by himself as he headed up the road toward the main house. Well, there was the dog, but she'd planned for that mutt. In fact, her desired outcome was probably already in progress. Tizzy had experienced first-hand the effects of Xanax's fast-acting formula. Within fifteen minutes of Cosmo eating his sedative-laced kibble, he'd be staggering around like a drunk sailor and unable to stop her. Good thing she stashed her unused prescription refills. Tizzy licked her lips in anticipation of the chaos she was about to unleash. Chills covered her arms as she peered through the grove of live oak and cedar elm trees, providing her the perfect cover to eavesdrop on her prey.

Mariah made her choice, albeit the wrong choice, and she'd pay with her life. But her memory would live on. Tizzy's transformation was almost complete. She gave herself a mental pat on the back for employing her genius as a technology wiz to forge all the necessary documents to assume Mariah's identity.

She fingered the turquoise earrings her roommate treasured as they dangled from her ears, then giggled as she murmured the adage, "If you can't beat 'em, join 'em."

Tizzy shifted her backpack for access to a side pocket, careful not to stab herself with the bowie knife, unsheathed for easy access, and retrieved a pair of high-powered, military-grade binoculars. With a slight adjustment of the lens as she peered from her vantage point into the side window, her primary target came into focus. Mariah, her blonde hair sweeping her shoulders, wore a thin, V-neck t-shirt that skimmed her butt cheeks as she peered out the cabin's living room window. A twinge of regret taunted her psyche. The stunning blonde was damn near the perfect woman but to her credit, she never used her beauty, which rivaled that of a Nordic goddess, and relied only on her smarts to advance in a male-dominated profession. She clucked with disappointment. John was to blame. If he hadn't stolen Mariah's attention, it would have belonged to her. Their relationship would have progressed, and these actions wouldn't be necessary. She caught a motion next to Mariah and pivoted the glasses. A German Shepherd, similar in color to Cosmo but smaller, was chowing down on the bowl of kibble meant for Cosmo. *Well, I didn't count on that wrinkle but I'm glad I doused the entire bag.*

Tizzy released the binoculars and allowed them to hang loosely around her neck while she jogged back to the car. With the touch of a button, she popped open the trunk and heaved the large gas canister onto the ground. On her way to the cabin, she'd discovered an ideal hiding place for the container in the bottom of a carved-out oak tree. Crouched as she crept along the wooded perimeter, she hid the gas cans and made a beeline for the kennels, careful to remain in the shadows. As she passed the guest house, the back door swung open, and Mariah stepped outside accompanied by the German Shepherd.

"Quite a chill in the air tonight my friend." She

motioned for the dog to do her business.

Tizzy squatted in place, barely breathing in an effort not to alert the dog to her position, but the bitch headed straight for her. She rustled through the bushes, moving ever closer. Tizzy peeked over the line of shrubs and witnessed the dog weaving, her eyes droopy.

Won't be long now.

Then, the thud of the door as it closed, permeated the quiet night. Another minute passed before she slowly rose to peek over the bushes. The dog lay on her side with her tongue lolled out of her mouth.

Tizzy snorted. *One down.*

Picking up her pace, she jogged straight to the entrance of the kennel, but John's voice stopped her. She ducked behind the corner of the building and eavesdropped. The stupid cripple instructed his K9 to fetch a food dish. A smile spread across her lips, and she gloated. The rapid clink, clink, clink of kibble dropping into a stainless-steel bowl was music to her ears. Cosmo would gobble it down and be incapacitated in a matter of minutes. With Mike out of town, they'd made it easy for her to pick the lock and sneak Xanax into the bag of dry dog food.

"That fuck you enjoyed earlier won't compare to how fucked you're both going to be when I'm finished," she muttered.

She peered around the corner of the building. John and Cosmo were both inside the run, near the back. Cosmo appeared to be sniffing at his food bowl. *Perfect.* She glanced around and found the perfect tool; a two-foot piece of rebar that would fit perfectly in the gate latch, blocking their exit. With a quick thrust, she secured the entrance. Out of nowhere, Cosmo charged the gate, snarling and barking. John screamed her name as he wheeled toward the entrance. She stayed long enough to laugh hysterically at their unescapable plight, then charged down the hill toward her finale.

****

Driven by a cocktail of anger and fear, John wormed his fingers through the chain links to joggle the rebar loose while Cosmo, triggered by the stench of his master's adrenaline-driven sweat, paced back and forth along the fence, pausing to scratch furiously at the shallow space between the fence and concrete. The dogs inside the kennel barked in response to Cosmo's thunderous warning. John hoped the commotion would alert Mariah, but the dogs were housed at the rear of the property to limit the noise for ranch guests. It was a long shot. One he couldn't count on. He had to find a way out. His phone. He'd left it in the supply room.

"Cosmo, here." The dog obeyed and sat expectantly at John's feet. "Phone. Fetch."

The German Shepherd shot down the length of the run as if fired out of a cannon and within seconds returned and dropped the phone in John's lap. He tapped speed dial for Mariah, silently commanding her to answer but after three rings, the call converted to voice mail, meaning she had it on mute. He hit his forehead with the phone while her recorded message played, painfully aware every second mattered. A shiver consumed his body as his mind filled with images of Mariah lying lifeless in a pool of blood. He squeezed his eyes shut, willing the images away. *Focus, John. Work the problem.* The phone's beep jerked him into action.

"Tizzy's here. Get your gun and lock yourself in

211

the bedroom with Artemis," he said, overemphasizing every word.

Next, he called Mike. "Bro, hell is raining down here at the ranch. What's your ETA?"

"Forty-five minutes, tops. What's going on?"

"Make it thirty. Tizzy's here, full psycho. She's locked me and Cosmo in the kennel. Going after Mariah."

"On my way. I'll call the sheriff and hope we won't need it, an ambulance."

"Thanks, man. Tizzy's the only one who'll need an ambulance once I get out of here."

"Copy that. Check the supply shed at the back of the kennel. I keep a pair of industrial-strength bolt cutters in there in case a wild animal gets trapped in the fence. Cut your way out."

John hung up and, within a minute, located the cutters. "Exactly what I need."

Stationed in front of the gate, he cut six strands of wire and made a hole large enough to get his hand and arm through the fence. He positioned his chair firmly against the fence for leverage. Then, he used all his hard-earned upper body strength to power himself high enough to remove the rebar. He unlatched the gate and faced the road as a swirl of grey smoke drifted up the hill from the direction of the guest house. Panic locked up his body. He feared almost nothing since his accident. The almost was his terror of being trapped in a burning building with the hot ashes burning his skin on contact and the heavy smoke choking out his ability to breathe. He'd been locked in his sister's barn by her ex-boyfriend and almost died from smoke inhalation while trying to free the horses also trapped inside.

Gavin had risked his life to save John, but the memory lingered like a hot ember. The swirl of smoke began to billow. He steeled himself against the threat. His life meant nothing without her in it.

"Cosmo, SEEK." The dog whined in protest, not wanting to leave his master but after circling the wheelchair twice bulleted down the road and out of sight.

****

Emboldened by the idea she'd outsmarted her opponent, Tizzy intermittently ran and skipped down the hill to the tree where she'd stashed the gas can. She approached the guest house with care, but Mariah was nowhere in sight. When she tried the screen door, it was latched. She slid her bowie knife from the leather sheath on her belt and slashed an opening large enough to poke her hand through and lift the hook. *Easy-peasy.* She turned the handle on the back door, and it opened. *Thanks, dummies.* She tilted her head and listened for a few seconds. Music blared from the bathroom. *Gotcha.* Tiptoeing across the living room, she deposited the gas can and crept toward the bathroom, picking up a rolling pin off the kitchen counter on her way through the house. As she passed the hallway table, she noticed a phone light up with an incoming call. John's name appeared on the screen. Tizzy smirked and grabbed the phone, tossing it in the drawer.

She made her way to the bathroom and noticed the door was cracked open. She glanced into the room and observed Mariah bent over the water spigots, using the palm of her hand to test the temperature.

With a deep breath and determination, Tizzy stepped behind Mariah and raised the pin above her head, aiming to deliver a fatal blow. Mariah spun around. Her eyes widened in alarm.

"Tizzy!" The pin descended and struck a glancing blow against Mariah's temple. She grabbed the towel rack as she collapsed, yanking it, along with chunks of plaster, from the wall. The amount of blood running down Mariah's face would have alarmed anyone else but not Tizzy. A snicker curled her lips.

"You should have picked me." She spat on Mariah then positioned the rolling pin over her target's face in preparation for a death blow but hesitated, then released the handle. The heavy wood thunked against Mariah's nose.

"That'll leave a bruise." She said as she backed out of the bathroom and down the short hallway to the gas can. Excited to get things rolling, she searched the room for the best fuel and settled on a wool throw.

Unexpected barking at the back door startled her, so she scurried to the front exit, tipping the gas can over, and hesitating long enough to drop a lit cigarette lighter.

"Burn baby burn," she muttered as she fled out the front door toward the safety of her car.

She only had a short distance to cover, but Cosmo's growl grew closer and within seconds the snapping of powerful jaws propelled her faster despite the burn in her lungs.

"That fucking dog just won't die." She scrambled into her car, out of breath, and slammed the door, almost catching Cosmo's nose. Undeterred, the dog braced his front paws on the closed window, baring his teeth between growling barks. Tizzy hit the reverse button and stomped on the gas. As soon as the dog dropped to the ground, she shifted into drive and steered straight for him, clipping him in the shoulder with her front bumper.

"Take that, you fucking mutt," she said, checking her rear-view mirror as he limped erratically toward the house and the glow of flames illuminating the windows.

"Good riddance, losers."

She fishtailed onto the dark country road. *By the time help arrives, they'll be dead, and I'll be seated comfortably in first class on a jet headed for Cuba via Canada.*

****

Desperation clouded John's mind, but his powerful forearms spun the wheels of his chair in a fast rhythmic motion, consuming the distance to the guest house and his love. He called for Cosmo. Silence. He whistled. Nothing. Visions of Cosmo and Mariah lying next to each other, dead, erupted in his head. Nausea swept his body. His chest tightened with panic while fear crawled under his skin. As he neared the front of the house, the smell of smoke accosted his nose and made it hard to breathe. His eyes watered from the sting as he tested the doorknob for heat. Finding it still cool to the touch, he twisted and then flung open the front door where he was greeted with an intense burst of hot air. He recoiled, but his drive to save Mariah overpowered the instinctive cringe.

He leaned forward and yelled. "Mariah, Mariah!" A sob choked his scream. "Mariah." The intensity of the heat swelled his tongue and parched his throat.

A wet nose touched his hand. "Cosmo." Relief showered his body. "You okay, buddy?"

Cosmo lifted his paw and whimpered as blood

trickled down his leg. John stroked the leg. "Thank God. Nothing's broken." He cupped Cosmo's jaw and drew him to eye level. "You still in the fight?" Cosmo answered with a loud bark and pointed his nose toward the back of the house.

"Cosmo, find Mariah," John said between coughs. The dog dropped his head and disappeared behind the grey veil of smoke. Triggered by the memory of being trapped in a burning barn, John fought to reduce his panic to a dull roar. Gavin wasn't here. Mike was miles away. If something went sideways…. He gritted his teeth. It already had. He prayed Mariah was still alive. He edged his chair closer to the rubber threshold and, with his right arm covering his nose and mouth, thrust the chair through the opening. Cosmo's frantic bark directed him to the back of the house where the flames hadn't yet spread.

She appeared so still, motionless, and quite possibly, dead. His heart thudded with an unpleasant, irregular beat as Cosmo licked her face in long, even strokes. She stirred, then moaned. Cosmo whimpered in between continued licks and began tugging at her arm.

"Mariah, baby. I'm here. We gotta get you out of here, pronto." The heat of the fire grew closer by the second and he realized flames would block their exit in a matter of minutes.

Her eyes opened and tried to focus on him. "John, thank God." Mariah moaned when she touched her head, "It was Tizzy."

"I know. She won't get far." He wheeled as close to her as he could. "Use the frame of my chair to lift up."

She latched her arm on the chair and strained to

216

rise but fell back. "I can't."

John winced at the amount of blood pooled on the floor. "Cosmo will help you."

As if he understood every word, Cosmo snagged the back of her collar and tugged her to a slight incline, enough for John to gain leverage and haul her into his lap. She limply swung her arm around his neck and steadied her head of red-matted hair on his shoulder.

"There you go," he said with a gentle squeeze, aware the blood from her head had soaked his shirt. "Let's get you out of here." *So much blood. Got to get you to a hospital posthaste.*

His stomach dropped when he entered the living room and spotted flames sprawled from the cloth sofa along the line of gasoline to the front door, blocking their exit. Cosmo circled the chair several times with dizzying speed before reversing course toward the back door. Thick smoke curtained the room and John lost sight of Cosmo, but he'd learned to trust the dog with his life. With one hand on Mariah to brace her against him, he wheeled around and blindly followed the excited yips until the smoke thinned then cleared and he found himself at the back door. Cosmo had charged through the screen on the back door and escaped down the ramp, leading them to safety.

"I love that dog more than life itself," he said as he hurried down the ramp to the backside of the house and away from the direction the wind blew the smoke.

"Augh," Mariah moaned. "Everything hurts."

"Breathe, baby," he said as he lifted Mariah's chin, then inhaled a deep volume of fresh air himself. Not sure if the house would explode, John scanned the area for the presence of a gas tank as he scooted to the far end of the paved driveway. Positioned a safe distance from the house, he gathered Mariah in his arms and hugged her tight.

"How are you holding up?" With delicate strokes, he outlined the emerging bruise on her shoulder.

"I'm holding." She groaned, then continued. "My head is exploding." She raised her squinted gaze to meet John's and gasped. "Artemis." Her eyes widened. "I let her out to do her business. Oh god, John. She didn't come back?"

"We'll find her. Don't worry." He searched the darkness for signs of the female shepherd while intermittently beckoning her with a strained whistle until the blare of sirens grabbed his attention. As the first responders closed the distance, they filled the silence with louder and more frequent horn screeches. Their nightmare wasn't over, but he welcomed the assistance.

"Help is on the way," he said with a relieved heave of his shoulders. He strengthened his grip on Mariah and whispered, "We'll find Artemis."

"Is Cosmo okay? Where is he?" She tried to raise her head but winced.

Cosmo. He hadn't seen the dog since he escaped down the back ramp.

"Cosmo, come," he said, his voice low and gravelly from the scratch of smoke inhalation. He twisted around but the K-9, who usually responded instantly to his command, was nowhere in sight.

"Cosmo, where are you, buddy?" He repeated the plea with as much volume as his raw throat would allow, then listened for a croaky bark or a whimper or even a rustle in the bushes if the smoke had damaged the dog's vocal cords too. Mariah's labored breathing, along with his own heavy inhales filled the space in a disturbing duet. Cosmo was MIA.

"He's not answering. Something's wrong." John adjusted his hold on Mariah, then trundled toward the woods, calling softly, "Cosmo, come."

Out of the darkness, Cosmo appeared, advancing with an uncharacteristic lumber, wheezing, and coughing, his breathing labored, then once alongside John, collapsed.

"Oh god, no!" John cried out, dragging both hands down his face. "He needs help."

Mariah grasped the arms of the chair and struggled to stand but John's grip remained firm. "You have a head wound. Sit still."

"My adrenaline kicked in. I can handle this and he's in critical condition. Let me go." She pleaded with him as she wrestled free from his grip. "I know first aid."

John weighed the consequences of allowing Mariah to become mobile against Cosmo not receiving immediate aid. He nodded and helped Mariah angle her body off the chair and onto the ground in a kneeling position, where she placed her ear on Cosmo's chest and listened for a heartbeat.

"Status?" John curled forward and gripped the arms of his chair.

"Not breathing," she answered then started mouth-to-mouth resuscitation on the motionless K-9, clamping his mouth shut and rhythmically breathing into his nose.

Life without Cosmo triggered a fear of reliving the unbearable void that existed before he entered John's life. There was nothing he could do to salve the hopeless throb of his heart but shore up against the potential loss and pray. Not a religious man, he lowered his head anyway and asked for this one small favor. Let the dog live.

A blast of sirens cut through his meditation and when he lifted his head, headlights pierced the dark path. Tires screeched and gravel spewed as Mike's truck slammed to a stop, followed by a fire truck and an ambulance. He exited shouting orders. John couldn't hear the words, but Mike's actions exhibited his strong resolve to convert chaos to order. Always one to assert himself into the middle of a firefight, his first action was to direct the ambulance personnel. A paramedic scurried over to Mariah and relieved her by placing an Ambubag over Cosmo's nose while a second one examined Mariah's head. Next, he played traffic cop and instructed the firefighters where to park their engines. John assumed another engine plus a tanker was on the way and Mike recognized that a blocked road could blow up their ability to assault the fire. For the first time tonight, John experienced a sense of relief as Mike rushed to his side.

"I've never been so happy to see your ugly mug," John said to Mike, half crying, half laughing as his friend embraced him.

"Jesus, man. What the fuck happened?" Mike asked. He emitted a low whistle while he examined the chaotic scene dotted with firemen dousing the remaining flames, a paramedic checking Mariah's vitals, and another administering oxygen to Cosmo.

"Tizzy happened." John ground out the words. "I underestimated her. This is on me."

"Whoa, dude" He raised his hands in a stop gesture. "This is NOT on you. I pegged her for a run-of-the-mill psycho incapable of executing sociopathic level strategy, but this chick is off the charts." He lowered his hands to John's shoulders. "Bottom line. She won't get far."

John nodded, casting his gaze to his feet. "I'll make good on the damage to your house."

"It's insured and I doubt the damage is as bad as it appears. The floors are stone as is the exterior for the very reason fires this far out in the country are devastating due to the time it takes for help to arrive."

"You're just trying to make me feel better."

Mike snorted. "I would never do that, bro."

"Asshole."

"That's more like it," Mike said, gesturing in the direction of Mariah and Cosmo. "Looks like Cosmo's awake and Mariah's resisting the efforts of the paramedic to load her onto the ambulance."

Mike glanced around and scratched his head. "Where's Artemis?"

"I don't know and that worries me. Mariah let her out to do her business right before this shitstorm started. Now, she's vanished. Even in all the noise and with me calling her, no response." John shook his head. "You think Tizzy…?"

"Don't go there, bro. Artemis is clever and suspicious of strangers. We'll find her. It's possible all the commotion scared her, and she ran off." He tapped John's knee. "I'll initiate a search party and we'll find her. But first, I'm gonna run Cosmo over to my vet for a checkup. You get the easy job of helping that poor SOB convince Mariah she needs to go to the hospital."

****

John gazed at Mariah as she rested on a hospital bed behind a curtained enclosure in the emergency room. Her pose, with eyes closed and arms crossed over her chest, resembled a dead body in a coffin and after the checklist of tests she'd been subjected to, one could wonder if she dreamed of that eternal slumber. With a feather's touch, he grazed her arm with the backs of his fingers and shivered at the thought of how close he'd come to losing her, to the pose being permanent.

"I'm awake," she said, squinting at him with one eye open.

"And alive, thank God." He smiled, despite the definite tremble in his bottom lip.

"I'm tough, my love." She attempted to ball both fists and imitate the stance of a boxer, but the IV line halted her forward motion. "Ouch!"

"Careful. I don't want you in here one minute longer than you need to be."

"Oh, don't you worry. I have a fugitive to pursue, catch, and throttle." Her face twisted into an angry scowl.

Mike peeked his head into the room. "No, you don't. I'm happy to report 'Little Miss Chaos' was apprehended at the airport boarding a plane to Canada."

"Well, that was dumb." A deep frown furrowed John's brow. "We have extradition with Canada."

"But not with Cuba, her final destination." Mike tapped his finger against his head.

Mariah propped herself up on her elbows. "Where are they taking her?"

"If looks could kill, Tizzy would be long-distance dead," John said, seething, as he crossflowed the daggers darting across the room from Mariah to Mike.

Mike stepped back and raised his right hand, palm out. "Listen, sister, law enforcement can handle this."

"Not with the same enthusiasm I would." She huffed, then sank back on the pillow.

John decided Mike's diplomacy with Mariah far exceeded anything he could offer to dissuade her. With a discreet hand signal, he motioned for his SEAL buddy to take point.

Mike acknowledged with a tip up of his chin. "I have no doubt about that." He didn't miss a beat as he lowered his hand and stepped forward, a smile plastered across his face. "You'll get your chance to face her in court when you're healed. Don't give her the satisfaction of seeing you hurt."

"Good point." Mariah cast her eyes upward as if contemplating the encounter.

Well played, my man. John had always admired Mike's finesse with the ladies.

"Any update on Artemis?" John cast a worried glance at Mariah.

Mike started to answer but Mariah interrupted him. "Yes, Artemis. Where's my girl?" She crossed her arms. "The last time I remember seeing her was when I let her out to pee and she disappeared into the woods." She sighed. "Then all hell broke out."

"Good news on that front. The search party found her passed out in the woods from an apparent overdose of an unknown drug."

Mariah gasped and clutched her chest. "But she's okay?"

"Yes. No physical signs of abuse or trauma. She woke up next to Cosmo at the vet's office and wagged her tail when she recognized me."

"Thank goodness." She heaved a deep sigh. "We need to make sure animal abuse charges get tacked on to Tizzy's list of crimes."

"How's Cosmo doing?" John asked.

"He's tough like his dad. No broken bones. His leg is badly bruised and tender but will heal."

"What about the smoke inhalation?" He held his breath in anticipation of the answer.

"The vet pumped him full of oxygen and cleaned out his lungs but told me he might have a cough for a while before he's good as new."

John's chest tightened and his throat constricted as relief from the silent worry poured through every cell of his body. Afraid he would openly sob if he tried to talk, he squeezed his eyes shut but a single tear trickled down his cheek. He subtly swiped at it with the back of his hand. *Too late*. Mariah extended her arm across the metal frame and clasped his hand while Mike embraced him in a full bro hug. He lost control. Sobs shook his body as he choked out the words, "I'd be lost without that dog." Mariah kissed his hand and raised it to her cheek. Mike increased his embrace and patted John's back. Raw emotion replaced all his shields, the ones he held firmly in place. The ones that aided him in refusing counseling after his combat injury so he wouldn't have to confront the permanence of the disability. They'd hardened his defenses against rejection for not being whole. Cosmo had allowed him to be whole again. Together they were one.

"Go ahead, buddy. Let it rip. We're here for you," Mike whispered.

"We got you, my love," Mariah cooed.

The epiphany swept him with the suddenness of a haboob in the Arizona desert. His injury didn't define him. He'd achieved past the physical limitation, but most importantly, he was loved, by good people. The best people and a dog.

Chapter Twenty-Seven

Two months later

A week had passed since John returned to Ocala, but she missed him. Her heart ached when she pictured his boyish face as he backed down the driveway, Cosmo in the front seat beside him and Artemis barking her head off from the back seat. He'd been her rock, no, more like an entire rock garden during the trial. Convinced his testimony reversed Tisdale's insanity plea into prison time, she'd said yes to living on his side of the Mississippi with the only condition being her mother would join them. He understood and enthusiastically agreed with Kathleen's relocation to the farm. She stayed behind to help her mother sell off what she no longer needed and then pack for the movers. The few personal possessions still in one piece after Tizzy's demolition derby on her apartment were already packed and sitting in a POD at Mike's house. Despite the fact she loved her job and had close friends in the local game warden district, once John presented his reasons for Ocala to be their permanent home, she conceded. The value of his services as an expert witness in Florida could not be understated. His clients, along with law enforcement, counted on him in the prosecution of animal cruelty cases, home invasion cases, and other sordid felony crime cases.

Giving her notice had been hard, harder than she imagined. She didn't expect Frank and Tommy to become emotional but the memory of Frank as he cleared his throat then hugged her and Tommy when he punched her arm then swiped tears from his face would last forever in her heart. In the days that followed her notice, they lightened up and ribbed her about being lovestruck and teased her they'd finally get some peace and quiet around the office with her gone. In the end, they wished her well.

Mariah kissed her mother's cheek, then stepped back. "I really appreciate you letting me stay here while Mike's house is getting repaired."

"Oh, darling daughter, you're always welcomed." She smiled. "You've been through so much these past few months." She fussed with the ends of Mariah's hair before wrapping her arms around her daughter's waist and burying her face in the soft, furry fabric of Mariah's sweater.

"Are you crying?" Mariah patted her mother's back.

"No," she mumbled, burying her head deeper in the layers of the purple angora.

Mariah clasped her mother's arms and leaned her back, searching her face. "Liar," she said, smiling. "I'm safe and totally recovered."

"I know, sweetheart, but when you and John told me the details about Tizzy, I realized how close I came to losing you." Tears flooded her eyes and dripped down her chin. "I could have lost you." She clutched the bottom of her apron and used it as a handkerchief. "It pains me to know how much you were dealing with all alone." Her shoulders quivered.

"I wasn't alone, Mama." She helped dab the wet spots on her mother's cheek. "John had my back."

"I'm grateful beyond words for that man. I simply had no idea how much things had escalated. Why didn't you tell me?" She snuffled.

"I didn't want to worry you, Mama. Besides, I'm a grown woman, capable of handling life's challenges and bad actors. And now I have the best man on the planet to share it all with."

"I had no doubt you'd say yes." She beamed. "I love John too, my sweet girl."

Kathleen glanced at Alice. "I guess now is as good a time as any to have a mother-daughter talk."

"About what?"

"The future. Mine and yours." She plopped into her easy chair. "I'm staying here when you relocate to Ocala."

"How did you know I agreed to move to Florida?"

"Because, my dear, that's the smartest decision for both you and John. His business and family are all there."

"True but *my* family's here." She hand-signed a heart and smiled. "Besides, I agreed only if you'd come with us. That's the one condition I gave John."

"I understand." She gave a second glance to Alice, who stepped next to Kathleen in apparent support. "I've given this a whole lot of mindful consideration. I'm staying here." She interlocked her fingers and dropped her hands in her lap. "Alice has offered to be my full-time caretaker. This house and neighborhood are familiar to me. I still have friends here and even though Franny decided to relocate to Arizona. I'm closer to her if I stay here than if I relocate to Florida." She locked eyes with Alice who rested a hand on her shoulder.

Taken off guard by her mother's unwavering stance, Mariah simply nodded, glancing between Alice and her mother while collecting her thoughts about where to go from here. They'd obviously rehearsed the spiel to a debate level with Alice in full league on the decision. When she hired Alice, she never expected the relationship to be a long-term solution, but apparently the two had hit it off. Grief swept Mariah. *Had Alice replaced her?* She swallowed hard and stepped forward, prepared for a verbal battle, driven by the protective impulse she'd acquired after her father died, but when she opened her mouth, the words choked in her throat. Arguing the decision with her Irish mother was useless. Stubbornness ran in the family and when she gazed at the firm set of her mother's mouth, she realized even if she won the argument, she'd lose in the long term by damaging their relationship. Her mother deserved to be happy for whatever time she had left. Mariah could and would give her that.

"I'll let John know I'm staying here." She hoped her poker face held because the mix of emotions flooded her senses with random chaos.

"No, you won't. John and I had time to get to know each other when I helped him buy your ring and I know about the plot of land on the farm where you two will build your dream house."

"Mother, you're my responsibility and I won't abandon you."

"You're not abandoning me. I'm making a fully informed decision." She beckoned Mariah closer. "Go live a beautiful life. I'll be fine. If things change here, I'll agree to consider Ocala." She cupped Mariah's face in her hands. "I love you. This is what I want for myself." As if she had read Mariah's mind, she continued, "No one could ever replace you or the love I have for you."

Mariah fell to her knees and hugged her mother. "Promise we will FaceTime once a day."

Alice interrupted. "I promise."

Mariah glanced up at Alice and smiled. "I believe you."

"Now, young lady, I think you have some packing to do. Get going before I call your fire-breathing fiancé to rescue me from my over-protective daughter."

"I'm all set." Mariah kissed her mother's cheek and squeezed her shoulders, then stood to shake Alice's hand.

Alice folded her into an embrace and said, "I've got this."

Mariah had arrived at her mother's house with the single purpose of packing up and moving her. She departed with a new perspective. An inseparable bond existed between her and her mother. She had a new understanding of the importance of John being with his family and was relieved she hadn't forced John into the difficult decision of choosing. He didn't have to. No one should have to.

****

John and both K-9s received a hero's welcome from Gavin and Ariel after arriving back in Ocala. He figured he, at least, had hundreds of good behavior chits in reserve after filling them in on the Texas saga that almost got him, both dogs and Mariah killed. He twirled back and forth in his chair as he reflected on the past ten weeks. *What a whirlwind.* His lip curled and he exhaled a chuffed grunt as he recalled the explosive deposition where he told the defending attorney to shove Tizzy's insanity plea where the sun never shines.

Then, on the first day of the trial, he observed the same attorney's smug smile vaporize as Mariah's entire unit showed up in uniform. They filed in and filled the first two rows behind her. *I think that sycophant weasel of an attorney pissed his pants.*

A twinge of guilt pervaded his conscience. He fully understood what having someone's back meant so taking her away from such a devoted bunch of guys bothered him, but he tucked the guilt away when he realized she'd elicit that kind of devotion wherever she landed.

If a job with the Florida Wildlife Commission was what his future wife decided, he'd support her decision. Her physical injuries had healed without complication but what worried him were the emotional scars. During the trial, he'd found her in the bathroom sobbing more than once. She'd admitted she wanted to kill Tizzy when their eyes met for the first time during the trial. It wasn't simply her maniacal presence but the academy award-level innocent act she put on for the jury that drove Mariah's anger and frustration. He struggled to maintain control for his woman but when the little psycho whined, 'I just wanted you to notice me,' while she swiped at a faked tear, he lost his shit and screamed, 'You didn't get your way. You'll never have her.'

The judge gave a stern warning, threatening that if he had one more outburst, he'd be charged with contempt. He replied in the affirmative but internally seethed how not sorry he was.

Betrayal was a bitch. Trust with anyone new would be a challenge for Mariah. That's where Artemis figured in. He'd gotten her officially certified as a service dog so she could accompany her master anywhere, including work if she decided to join the Florida game wardens. But she didn't have to worry about Tizzy. The jury hadn't bought her act. She'd been found guilty and received a sentence of twenty-five years in prison.

A soft knock on the door interrupted Cosmo's afternoon nap. He lifted his head and shot a quick glance at John before uncurling and ambling to the door. He smelled through the small crack at the bottom and wagged his tail.

"It's open, sis."

Ariel peeked her head in. "Artemis is in labor." The corner of her lips curled. "Would the doggie daddy like to witness the birth?" She passed through the door and rubbed Cosmo's raised head. "We know you're the real pappa."

"Oh, man. You bet I would. Is she in the barn?"

"No, I have a comfy birthing area set up in my home office." She made a heart sign in the air. "She deserves special treatment as a family member. Have you told Mariah?"

"I wanted it to be a surprise." He laughed. "And leverage to get her here if needed." He tapped his temple with his right index finger.

"You're sneaky, little brother, but I do get it." She tapped her heart with her index finger. "We want her here as much as you do."

John raised an eyebrow. "Not possible."

His phone dinged, indicating a new text had

arrived. He smiled as he read it, then gazed up at his sister.

"Your main squeeze?" she asked, wrapping her arms around her waist.

"Very funny and you know she's my *only* squeeze." His gaze returned to the phone as a second ding chimed. He spoke aloud as he read. "She's packed and has the movers lined up for next week." His smile transformed into a frown.

"What?" Ariel said.

"Her mom isn't coming. That was the one condition she gave me on moving here. Her mother had to agree to move here."

"Well, they apparently worked it out."

"I need to call her and find out what happened." He rubbed his hand over his face. "I don't want her moving here with any regrets."

"Time for a bribe. Pull out all the stops and video the puppies."

"I was kidding earlier about using them as leverage. I had already decided to video the newborns for her so she could be a part of the experience."

He quickly typed a response to her text. —I want to hear all about the latest. Let's talk tonight.— He followed it with several emojis going from smiling to hearts to kisses, hit send, then placed his phone on the desk. He studied the screen for a minute before flipping it face down and exiting the office. His sister waited for him at the bottom of the ramp, palms flat against her breasts, shifting from one foot to the other. As he rolled next to her, she grimaced.

"Time to pump some milk," she said as she did an about-face. With a hurried wave of her arm, she scurried toward the main house. "Another reason I lodged Artemis in my office."

"What can I do to help?" John asked, keeping pace with the increased speed of her gait.

Ariel texted a quick message and then explained, "I've asked Rob to check in on Artemis and babysit until I get there. You join him."

"What if something goes wrong?" The undulating in his stomach annoyed him.

Ariel halted and grabbed the arms of his chair. "She's young, in perfect health, and has maternal instinct." She patted his knee. "And we have three to twelve hours before the first puppy thrusts himself into the world. This," —she pointed to her breasts— "will be done in twenty minutes."

"You'd give Wonder Woman a run for her money," he called out as she lightly jogged up the back door stairs.

Chapter Twenty-Eight

Two weeks later

Winter, for most people across the United States, summoned up images of frigid weather, deep snowdrifts, and traffic snarls. Even Fort Worth, Texas where Mariah had lived most of her life, succumbed to freezing temperatures accompanied by wicked ice storms. So, the nonstop alerts and reports from the local Ocala weather channel about a frost warning with a possible one-night temperature drop to freezing amused her. She chuckled as she helped blanket the pricey thoroughbreds, rounded up from the pasture and herded into the barn for the night. Gavin was the one person on Wildwood Farm who treated the weather as a challenge, wearing cargo shorts and a long-sleeved flannel shirt with the sleeves rolled up to his elbows. She attributed his middle finger to the weather akin to his SEAL persona.

"Gavin, anything else you need help with to prepare for this bomb cyclone?" Mariah pretended a whole-body shiver.

"Yes, a nice hot toddy in front of the fireplace at the main house."

She continued to tease. "I thought that fireplace was just for decoration. You mean it works?"

"You jest," —he smirked— "but fire elicits

important primal instincts," —his gaze fell on Ariel— "like pleasure."

"I'm blushing," Ariel said, fanning her face. She blew Gavin a kiss. "Let's head up to the house. Rob built a nice fire." She pointed to John, who held Alexander in his lap "He looks good on you, little brother."

John snugged the baby's hoodie around his chubby face. "I'll be a married man in a few months with the added responsibility of my very own mother-in-law living on the property," —he winked at Mariah— "which I'm happy about." Time to drop the 'little' moniker."

"You're killing me, little brother." Ariel laughed.

"I'll make you a deal. I won't call my nephew, Elmo if you drop the 'little' and just call me John."

Ariel stepped next to Mariah and curled her arm inside of the other woman's. "What do you think, future sister-in-law?" She tightened the hold into a hug. "Should I continue to torture him or admit he's all grown up?"

Mariah cleared her throat of the hard lump blocking her words but not her emotions. She backed up from the group and faced them.

"Ya'll have made me feel so at home, here. Thank you." She turned toward Ariel. "He's the best man I've ever known with the hugest heart and bravest soul. My vote is no more 'little.'"

Cosmo, who had been lying peacefully next to his master, sat up and barked as if to offer his vote.

"That's four to one, my love," Gavin said with a chuckle, then rubbed Cosmo behind the ears.

John's face glistened with tears already fallen and

evaporated but he sent a huge, warm smile to Mariah. "And my soon-to-be wife received an offer letter today to be a badass game warden for the Northeast region, headquartered right in Ocala."

"Are you accepting the offer?" Gavin asked.

"Sounds awesome," Ariel said. "Short commute and working with those same guys you met at the conference."

Mariah glanced at John and noticed his smile had faded. He'd asked her to join him in his booming security business but had made it clear he'd fully support her career as a game warden if that's what she wanted.

"Haven't decided yet, but if I do accept, it'll be as a married woman."

"Yay. We have a wedding to plan," Ariel said with her hands fisted as she did a brief jig.

"Besides, Mama arrives in a week." Mariah heaved a sigh. "I don't know how much time I have left with her before she doesn't recognize me but I'm grateful she changed her mind." Grief welled up in her chest and forced her to change the subject. She cleared her throat. "I'm very thankful to all of you for making this move happen."

Gavin stepped forward and hugged Mariah. "You're one of us now. You're family."

While maintaining the embrace, Mariah reached for John's hand. He clutched it close to his heart and kissed her knuckles.

In unison, they traversed the path from the barn to the house and, despite the increasing chill in the air, the love that surrounded her created the warmth of a cashmere blanket. Her heart had found its home, forever in Ocala.

A word about the author...

Connie is a multi-published, award-winning author. With close ties to the Navy SEAL community, Connie's mission as a writer is to offer the reader a realistic portrayal of men who transfer their alpha tendencies and athletic prowess into serving a noble cause.

A former English teacher and corporate executive Connie holds a B.A. from East Carolina University. Although she spent many years in the corporate world, her first love has always been writing. She maintains a portfolio of songs, poems, and stories she wrote as early as ten. When she isn't creating new plots, Connie enjoys Zumba fitness and claims her best story ideas come to her while dancing the Salsa.

Connie lives near the Gulf Coast of Florida with her German Shepherd Dog and a cat who takes no prisoners.

Website http://www.connieyharris.com

Thank you for purchasing
this publication of The Wild Rose Press, Inc.

For questions or more information
contact us at
info@thewildrosepress.com.

The Wild Rose Press, Inc.
www.thewildrosepress.com